A · TREASURY · OF
PONY
STORIES

CHOSEN BY
Linda Jennings

ILLUSTRATED BY
Anthony Lewis

Kingfisher

CONTENTS

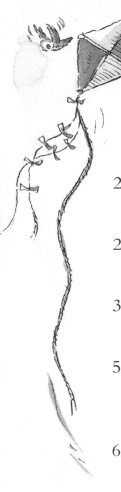

KINGFISHER • TREASURIES

Ideal for reading aloud with younger children, or for
more experienced readers to enjoy independently,
Kingfishe   or
children   ie
content   g.
There   id
fabl   he
worl   rs.

b   ıl
iı   ̣e
cł

KINGFISHER
An imprint of Larousse plc
Elsley House, 24-30 Great Titchfield Street
London W1P 7AD

First published by Kingfisher 1996
2 4 6 8 10 9 7 5 3 1

This selection copyright © Linda Jennings 1996
Illustrations copyright © Anthony Lewis 1996

The moral right of the authors, editor and illustrator has been asserted.

ISBN 1 85697 470 7

Printed in Great Britain

Acknowledgements

The publisher would like to thank the copyright holders for permission to reproduce the following copyright material:

Joan Aiken: A.M. Heath & Co. Ltd for "Managing Without the Moon" from *Mice and Mendelson* by Joan Aiken, Jonathan Cape 1978. Copyright © Joan Aiken 1978. **Marjorie Darke**: The author c/o Rogers, Coleridge & White Ltd for "Now You See Me, Now You Don't" by Marjorie Darke (copyright © Marjorie Darke 1979) from *The Cat-Flap and the Apple Pie*, compiled by Lance Salway. Copyright © W.H. Allen 1979. **Peter Dickinson**: Victor Gollancz Ltd for "Unicorn" from *Merlin Dreams* by Peter Dickinson. Copyright © Peter Dickinson 1988. **Ann de Gale**: Jennifer Luithlen Literary Agency for "Another Girl's Pony" by Ann de Gale. Copyright © Ann de Gale 1996. **Adèle Geras:** The author and Laura Cecil Literary Agency for "Nutmeg and Snowstorm" by Adèle Geras. Copyright © Adèle Geras 1996. **Laurence Housman**: Random House UK Ltd for "Rocking-Horse Land" from *Moonshine and Clover* by Laurence Housman, Jonathan Cape Ltd. Copyright © Laurence Housman. **Linda Jennings**: The author for "Patience" and "The Horses of the Sun". Copyright © Linda Jennings 1996. **Barbee Oliver Carleton**: Highlights for Children Inc. Columbus, Ohio for "A Hat for Crumpet" by Barbee Oliver Carleton. Copyright © Highlights for Children Inc. **Maggie Pearson**: The author for "The Horse of Fire and Thunder" by Maggie Pearson. Copyright © Maggie Pearson 1996. **Christine Pullein-Thompson**: Jennifer Luithlen Literary Agency for "Candy Stops a Train" by Christine Pullein-Thompson. Copyright © Christine Pullein-Thompson 1996. **Robert D. San Souci**: Dell Books, a division of Bantam Doubleday Dell Publishing Group Inc. for "The Hallowe'en Pony" from *Short and Shivery: Thirty Chilling Tales* by Robert D. San Souci. Copyright © Robert D. San Souci 1987. **Dinah Starkey**: Reed Consumer Books Ltd for "McGregor and the Kelpy" from *Ghosts and Bogles* by Dinah Starkey, William Heinemann Ltd. Copyright © Dinah Starkey 1987. **Julie Sykes**: The author for "Swallow" by Julie Sykes. Copyright © Julie Sykes 1996. **Ann Wigley**: Jennifer Luithlen Literary Agency for "Pony Island" by Ann Wigley. Copyright © Ann Wigley 1996.

Every effort has been made to obtain permission to reproduce copyright material but there may be cases where we have been unable to trace a copyright holder. The publisher will be happy to correct any omissions in future printings.

Managing Without the Moon

Joan Aiken

All the things I am going to tell you about happened more than a hundred years ago, in a big old park far to the north of England. This park – which was called Midnight Park – belonged to an old lord, who lived in a stable because his house had burned down. And in the park there also lived an old Orkney pony called Mr Mendelson. Mr Mendelson had two friends who were field-mice. And he was also lucky enough to have a piano, which the Old Lord had given him.

Mr Mendelson could not play the piano himself – who ever heard of a horse playing the piano? – but his friends the mice could play very well indeed, and so every evening they had a concert, and Mr Mendelson listened.

Besides beautiful music, Mr Mendelson was

particularly fond of the moon. He loved to watch it when, sometimes, in daytime, it floated across the sky like a white balloon, looking puzzled and lost, as if it were not sure of the way home. And, even better, Mr Mendelson loved the moon at night, when it shone bright as silver and made all the trees in the park throw long shadows across the grass. Every day Mr Mendelson's two friends, the fieldmice Bertha and Gertrude, used to spend several hours brushing and combing him all over, pulling the prickles and burrs out of his thick shaggy coat, plaiting his mane, teasing and stroking out his long tail with their tiny clever claws.

While the two mice tidied up Mr Mendelson they held long argumentative conversations.

The mice were much better informed than Mr Mendelson, because they sometimes went out of the park and under the town, in their tunnels, and they talked to the town mice and heard all the news. Whereas Mr Mendelson never went anywhere, now that he was so old; sometimes he just stood in one spot for hours together. But he thought a lot, all the time he was standing still.

"So what is the moon?" he asked Bertha one day, when she was brushing out his forelock.

The moon was floating overhead at the time, like a large white soap-bubble.

"The moon?" said Bertha, holding a tuft of forelock between her strong little claws, while she pulled out a thorn with her teeth and spat it away. "Pffft! Excuse me! The moon's a silver shilling."

"Excuse *me*!" said Gertrude, who was brushing Mr Mendelson's ears, "but the moon is *not* a silver shilling. It is a cream cracker. That's why it gets smaller all the time. Somebody is eating it up there. You could not eat a silver shilling."

"Pardon *me*: it is a shilling."

"*No*, Bertha. It is a plain biscuit."

"Whichever it is," said Mr Mendelson, "why doesn't it fall down?"

"Because the sky is sticky. Like honey."

"Sticky like jam," said Gertrude. Both mice were

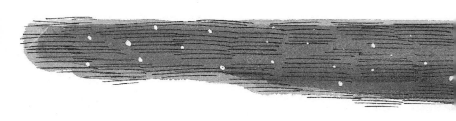

agreed about that. "The sky is so sticky that all kinds of things get stuck up there. Like sheep's wool on bramble bushes. In fact there *is* quite a lot of sheep's wool in the sky."

"That's true," said Mr Mendelson looking at the clouds floating past.

"There you are, Mr Mendelson! Now you're done for the day," said Bertha, sliding down his tail, while Gertrude gave a last polish to his shoes. "Go and look at yourself in the pond."

There was a tiny round pond in the park where Mr Mendelson lived with the mice. It was not much larger than a round table, and the grass came right to its edge.

Mr Mendelson walked slowly over to the pond and looked into it. There were some red and brown leaves floating about on the water, for autumn had come. Mr Mendelson could see his own reflection looking up at him. His coat was all black and shiny, because the mice had given him such a good brushing.

And then, suddenly, he saw something else in the pond.

"Bertha – Gertrude!" he called anxiously.

"Come here – quick! A bad thing has happened! The moon has fallen into the pond!"

Both mice came scampering to the water's edge and looked in. But now a whole patch of dead leaves had floated across the pond. There was nothing to be seen. The moon's reflection had gone.

"Oh, the moon has sunk down to the bottom, right into the mud!" mourned Mr Mendelson. "We shall never see it again."

He looked up at the sky, where clouds were beginning to gather. Sure enough, no moon was there.

"It will float up again," prophesied Gertrude. "Biscuits do float, after all."

"*No*, excuse *me*, Gertrude. It is a shilling, and shillings do *not* float."

That night it was very cold. Even inside his warm, thick coat, Mr Mendelson felt the cold in his old bones, and shivered in his sleep. Although the cold did not wake him, it made him dream. He dreamed about the gypsy, Dan Sligo, who lived in the woods on the edge of the park, and caught rabbits and cut clothes pegs and stole vegetables from people's gardens. Dan Sligo had a very clever lurcher dog called Jess, who was trained to pick up anything she found and take it back to her master. Jess had been taught to catch fish, too, and could snap a trout from the stream in her jaws without breaking a single one of its scales.

In the old pony's dream he saw Dan Sligo by the pond with a fishing-net; he saw the dog Jess dash into the water and come out with the moon in her teeth and give it to her master. Then the gypsy dropped the moon into his net and slung it over his shoulder and walked away.

"Oy moy, Dan Sligo has stolen the moon!" mourned Mr Mendelson in his sleep, and woke himself up. He was so cold, and so worried by his

dream, that although it was hardly morning yet, he made his way to the pond, which was some distance from where he had been sleeping with his chin resting on the keyboard of his beloved piano.

The weather was bitterly cold. As Mr Mendelson moved along, his hoofs went scrunch, scrunch, through the grass, which was white with frost.

When Mr Mendelson came close to the pond, what did he see? He saw Dan Sligo, with an axe, very busy, hacking away, all round the rim of the pond. The strokes of the axe made a loud splintering sound in the silent frosty park, which was all grey with early-morning light.

Dan Sligo saw the old pony coming slowly across the white crisp grass.

"How do, Mr Mendelson!" he called cheerfully. "Up early, ain't 'ee? Don't sleep so good these sharp nights, eh? Ancient bones gets to creaking in the frost, divvn't they? Best ask the Old Lord for a blanket."

"What are you doing, Dan Sligo?" asked Mr Mendelson. He was very worried at seeing the gypsy working by the pond where the moon lay drowned. His heart went geflip, geflap.

"What am I a-doing?" The gypsy winked. "Best ask Mr Brown the pastrycook how he makes his ice cream! A frozen tongue can't tell 'ee no lie, Mr Mendelson!"

And at that, Dan Sligo did an amazing thing. He gave a tilting push to the surface of the pond with his foot. He gave a pull with his arms. And the whole pond seemed to tip sideways in a great white circle. Dan Sligo tipped up the white circle on to its edge, and began to roll it away over the grass.

Mr Mendelson watched him go with starting eyes.

"Stop! Stop! Come back, Dan Sligo!" he called faintly. But the gypsy took no notice. He rolled his round of white over the grass to the park fence where he had a hand-barrow waiting, tipped forward on its wheel. He rolled the white circle straight into the barrow. And then he pushed the barrow away down the hill into the town.

When the two mice arrived, later in the morning, to brush Mr Mendelson's coat, they found the old pony very sad and silent.

"What's the matter, Mr Mendelson?" said Bertha, running up on to his nose, for his head hung down so low that it was an easy jump from a frosty clump of grass. "Why are you so gloomy?"

"Dan Sligo was here early this morning, and he has stolen the moon out of our pond, and rolled it away down the hill."

"You're pulling my tail!" gasped Gertrude. "Stolen the moon? Dan Sligo? Oy, what a scoundrel! Why has he done that?"

"Why ask why? That sneak would steal the egg from his mother's breakfast if he thought he could get it away without her noticing," said Bertha. "Of course he'll sell it to somebody. But who would buy the moon?"

"He said something about Mr Brown the pastrycook," said Mr Mendelson sadly. "He said, 'Ask Mr Brown how he makes his ice cream.' What do you think he meant by that? What *is* ice cream?"

Even the well-informed mice didn't know that. But they promised Mr Mendelson that they would find out, when they had finished tidying him for the day; they would go and visit their cousins Martha and Charlotte, who lived under Mr Brown's shop and made use of his cake-crumbs.

All day Mr Mendelson wandered sorrowfully about the park. It was a grey cloudy day, very cold. He hardly did more than nibble at the frosty grass. Many, many times he peered sadly into the pond. Often, often, he gazed up at the sky. But no moon was to be seen in either place.

At six o'clock the mice returned and climbed up Mr Mendelson's tail on to the piano, for it was time to play their evening concert. But first, Mr Mendelson was anxious to know what they had found out from their cousins.

"Well? Well? How *does* Mr Brown the pastrycook make his ice cream?"

"He has a big wooden machine, as big as a barrel, and he turns a handle round and round and round. And then he opens the top and scoops out the ice cream."

"Yes? So what is this ice cream?"

"Charlotte and Martha stole a crumb for us to

try. It is round and cold and white, and it melts on your whiskers before you have a chance to taste it," said Bertha.

"I'm afraid it's quite clear that ice cream is made from melted moon," sighed Gertrude.

"Oy, moy!" lamented Mr Mendelson. "We shall never see our beautiful moon again. Dan Sligo has stolen it and Mr Brown has ground it up and made it into ice cream."

The two mice looked at each other and shook their heads.

"For once, Mr Mendelson," said Bertha, "I'm afraid you are right."

They all sat grieving for the moon in silence. Then Gertrude said, "Well, tears won't fry pancakes. Let's play a bit of music and try to cheer up. Just because the moon is gone, is that a reason to mope?"

"No – you are right," said her sister. "We'll have to learn to manage without the moon."

And without waiting any longer, the two mice began scampering up and down the keyboard of the piano, pressing down the black notes and the white, using their noses, their feet, and even their

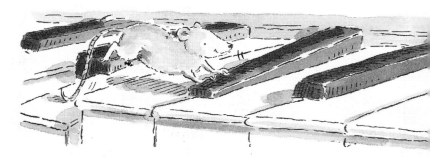

tails, with terrific dexterity and energy. They made such brilliant and glorious music that the Old Lord, who lived in the stables, heard it, and came rolling himself across the park in his wheelchair to listen and enjoy it at closer quarters.

"Now play the moonlight piece," said Mr Mendelson, when it was nearly time to stop.

The moonlight piece was his favourite, his particular favourite, for it was slow and thoughtful, moving along at a quiet dreamy pace like the moon gently drifting through the branches of trees, throwing one shadow after another.

As Mr Mendelson listened to it, a tear rolled down each side of his nose. He thought to himself, "I shall never see the moon again. The nights will always be dark from now on."

But then – all of a sudden – he noticed that the tears rolling down his nose each had a silvery dot of moon reflected in them. And when he raised his head, there was the moon itself, just climbing out of a hawthorn bush.

"Bertha! Gertrude!" he shouted. "Look! Look! The moon has come back! Your music must have put it together again!"

All three of them sat gazing in silent amazement as the moon disentangled itself from the bush and moved up into the sky.

Then the Old Lord said, "Well, well, it's my bedtime. And it's your bedtime too, Mr Mendelson. I brought your blanket tonight. Winter's just around the corner." And he buckled a warm tartan blanket around the old pony's barrel-stomach, before rolling himself away in his wheelchair.

"What did he mean, winter is just around the corner?" said Gertrude.

"Maybe he meant, just around the cornfield," suggested Bertha.

"Well anyway," said Mr Mendelson, "now we know for certain what the moon is made of. The moon is made of ice cream. And at least we know, too, that if Dan Sligo should steal it again, you can always get it back with your music."

So that night Mr Mendelson slept soundly in his blanket, without a single dream. And the mice slept soundly in their mouse-hole, which was warmly lined with combings from Mr Mendelson's thick coat.

Overhead, the moon drifted through the sky, and what it was made of, who can say?

Nutmeg and Snowstorm

Adèle Geras

Janet sucked the end of her pencil and thought about what she was going to write. How could she describe "My Pet" when she didn't have one? Dogs, cats, mice, hamsters and tortoises were not allowed in the flats, and there wasn't much to say about a couple of stick insects who used to live in a shoe-box with holes punched in the lid. Their names had been Zombie and Squash, but they didn't last very long, poor creatures, and even Janet hadn't felt like arranging a proper funeral for them. They'd ended up in one of the wheelie-bins at the back of the flats, still in their box, and that was that.

Janet put her hand up. "Please, Miss, I haven't got a pet." Miss Penfold pushed her glasses up her nose and sighed.

"Never mind, dear," she said at last. "Imagine a

21

pet. Tell us about a pet you would like to have if you could have one."

Janet bent her head. Now she knew exactly what to put. She began at once, worried that the bell would go before she could write about Nutmeg.

Last summer, we went on holiday to a farm. On the farm there was a pony called Nutmeg. She was quite small. She was brown with a white bit on her nose. On our last day, Mr Welling, the farmer, let me sit on Nutmeg and ride her. We walked all round a big field. I gave Nutmeg some sugar before we went home. I wish I could ride on Nutmeg's back again. I miss her. Mum says we can go to the farm again this year. I hope I can ride Nutmeg again. I wish I had a pony of my own. If I had a pony, I would look after it very well and brush its coat every day.

On her way home from school, Janet thought about Nutmeg. Once, she'd asked her mother:

"Why do I never dream about Nutmeg, Mum? I always think about her just before I go to sleep."

"Maybe you *do* dream about her," Mum said. "Maybe it's just that you can't remember the dream when you wake up."

What was the point of dreaming, Janet thought, if you couldn't remember anything in the morning? She decided to start daydreaming instead, and that was much better. If she concentrated very hard, it was easy to imagine exactly what it would feel like to ride Nutmeg round the field again; what it would be like to be so high up that you could look down at Mr Welling's bald patch; what the wind would sound like whistling round your ears. Janet had never told anyone, but secretly she pretended that Nutmeg was stabled in her cupboard, and each evening she opened the cupboard doors and fed her imaginary sugar lumps. Sometimes she brushed the sleeves of her winter coat with a pretend brush and played at grooming.

At Christmas, Janet's grandmother had given her a small china horse.

"You're pony-mad," she said, "so I thought you'd like this. Isn't it beautiful?"

"Yes," Janet had said, and the horse was beautiful, even though he wasn't a bit like Nutmeg. This horse was white all over and had a flying mane, and looked as though he were racing full-tilt across the top of the chest of drawers. Janet didn't play with her china horse. He was too fragile, for one thing, and for another, he looked too grand and dignified for pretending games.

That night, Janet dreamed that she was galloping across a sandy beach with the wind tearing at her hair; then she dreamed that she was riding through a forest on an enormous horse that wasn't Nutmeg at all. She clung to the white mane for dear life, ducking her head to avoid the lowest branches. It was like being on a fast ride at the fair: thrilling and terrifying all at once.

When she woke up, she was sad that the dream was over. It wasn't until she was telling her mum about it at breakfast that she realized . . .

"Mum," she said, "I think it was my white china

horse that I was riding in my dream. I'm sure it was."

"I expect so, dear," said Mum, but Janet could tell she wasn't really listening properly.

"I wish it was the summer holidays," Janet said. "I wish time would go quickly."

Time *did* go quickly. Janet and her mum arrived at the farm at four o'clock on a greyish August afternoon.

"It's going to rain," said Janet. "It's not like summer at all. Can we go and see Nutmeg first?"

"No," said Mum. "We'll go and put our things away first, and say 'hello' to Mr and Mrs Welling. Then we'll go and see where Nutmeg is."

Janet kept quiet all through the "hellos" and "how are yous?" and "what have you been up to since last years?" that grown-ups felt they had to go through before they could talk properly about anything. In the end, she couldn't contain herself for one more minute.

"Please, Mr Welling, where's Nutmeg? May I go and see her before we have tea?"

"Oh, my goodness," said Mrs Welling. "Didn't we tell you? Nutmeg has gone . . . she's moved to a farm in Cumbria . . . she was getting a bit long in the tooth for us. It's a sort of retirement home for horses . . . a lovely place, near a lake. I'm sure Nutmeg's very happy."

Janet couldn't help what happened next. She felt such a sadness all over that she let out a howl like a kicked puppy, and soon the tears were pouring down her face. She was crying so much that her words came out all hiccupy and wet and muddled.

"But I've missed her for a whole year," she sobbed. "I wanted to see her."

Mr Welling took out a big red handkerchief.

"Here," he said to Janet. "Blow your nose and wipe your eyes, and come along with me to the top field."

Janet wiped and blew and followed Mr Welling. They walked along in silence. The sun had pushed its way out from behind the grey clouds, but Janet still felt as if the inside of her head were full of black stones, all bumping about.

"Look over there," said Mr Welling, "under the plane tree." Janet looked. Then she looked again. There, standing quietly next to the fence, was the most beautiful white horse in the world. She blinked.

"That's Snowstorm," said Mr Welling. "You can ride him tomorrow. I'll walk round the field with you, first thing after breakfast."

"He looks . . ." Janet began.

"Yes?" said Mr Welling.

"Nothing," said Janet, but she knew that Snowstorm was the horse she had ridden in her dreams; a real, living version of the little china ornament that stood on the chest of drawers in her bedroom.

"I'm longing to ride Snowstorm," she said at last, "but I still miss Nutmeg. Don't you?"

"Of course we do," said Mr Welling, "but in a way, she's still here."

"Where?" Janet looked round, bewildered.

"Here," said Mr Welling, tapping his forehead with his fingers, "as long as we all remember her."

Janet went up to Snowstorm and stroked his smooth, white neck.

"Hello," she said, and Snowstorm snorted and tossed his head and looked at Janet almost as though he recognized her.

PATIENCE

A French tale retold by Linda Jennings

Patience belonged to the Queen. She was a small, gentle, honey-coloured pony, who had belonged to the Queen since she was a young princess. Patience was known for her good temper, and she had never kicked or bitten anyone in her life.

When Princess Florence became Queen and came to live in the royal palace, Patience came with her. The little pony was looked after by an elderly groom called Benjamin, who gave her the choicest pony nuts, and brushed her till her coat shone like velvet. She was too small for the Queen to ride any more, but the young Prince was growing from a baby into a toddler, and would soon be big enough to sit on Patience's back.

Then one day, Benjamin decided to retire. He

wanted to go to live with his daughter in the country, and much as he loved Patience, he decided to leave the big busy palace for ever.

"What shall we do?" the Queen asked her husband. "Who on earth could look after Patience as well as Benjamin did?"

"We will advertise," said the King, and for several weeks a stream of hopeful grooms arrived at the palace. For one reason or another, none of them was suitable. Some could not handle a pony without hitting it, and others had come along only because they wanted to look inside the palace.

Finally, the King said, "I have an idea. I have just taken on a young page who is a farmer's son. Surely *he* will know all about ponies?"

The Queen sent for the page, whose name was Jack. He was very young, but he did know all about horses.

"I looked after my dad's pony before I came here, your Majesty," he said. He smiled a big, cheerful smile, and the Queen was won over.

When the Queen took Jack to the stables, he did all the right things. He had brought along some rosy apples, and he fed them to Patience, one by one. He whispered gently into her ears. Patience stood there patiently, as usual, but she did not nuzzle into Jack's pockets and her ears drooped down.

"She's beautiful," said Jack, giving the Queen one of his big smiles.

"The job is yours, then," said the Queen.

Before Benjamin retired, he tried to show Jack exactly how to handle the little pony.

"She's as good as gold," he said. "Used to lots of love and kindness, that's why."

"All right, all right," said Jack impatiently. "I know all about horses, I do. No need to tell me anything."

Benjamin said goodbye to his favourite pony with a tear in his eye. He felt uneasy, though he could not have said why.

For the first few weeks, the Queen would turn up at the stables daily, to see how Jack was getting on with Patience. She liked what she saw. Patience's coat shone, and the stable was filled with the smell of leather polish.

"See how she loves me, your Majesty," said Jack, putting his arm around Patience's neck. But for some reason, Patience tossed her head and gave a sad little whinny.

Of course, thought the Queen, it will take time for her to get used to her new groom. Stands to reason.

But if the Queen had hidden out of sight, she would soon have seen what was upsetting Patience. At first the boy had been delighted to be employed by the Palace with a fine uniform and a good wage. But no sooner had he begun looking after the Queen's pony, than he became restless and bored.

"Stupid thing!" he cried. "There's no go in you. You've got no spirit."

He swung on to Patience's back, and hit her with a whip. Patience tossed her head, but did not move. Jack hit her again, and the bit jagged her tender mouth. She twitched a foot, but she did not throw him.

One day, Jack invited all the palace pages to the stables.

"I've thought up a game," he giggled. "It's called 'Getting Patience to Move'."

Poor Patience! The pages hit her, waved burning rags in front of her nose, tugged at her reins, and swung upside down from her stomach. But though her legs twitched, she did not kick them.

"Let's scare the ears off her, now!" cried Jack, and he took an old scarf and tied it round her eyes. Then all the laughing boys pushed and kicked poor Patience across the courtyard and towards the clock tower.

"Up you go," laughed Jack.

And up Patience went, up the little twisty staircase to the very top of the tower. All the pages pushed and shoved her from behind. The poor pony began to feel dizzy as she went round and round the spiral staircase. At last, she stumbled over the threshold at the top of the stairs, and, as Jack took off her blindfold, she found herself on a wide platform.

Where was she? She walked round the platform on trembling legs. Then she looked over the edge. Quite a crowd had gathered, laughing and shouting and pointing at the poor confused little pony high above them. By now, all the pages had vanished.

It took four men to coax Patience down the staircase again.

"However did she get up there?" someone asked. But no one guessed what had really happened.

Patience never forgot the fear or the shame of it all. Her legs twitched, as she thought of Jack's jeering face, and she knew the time had come to teach him a lesson.

The time was not long in coming, for the following week Jack and Patience were chosen to lead the Queen's Grand Birthday Procession.

When the day arrived, everyone oohed and aahed at the sight of the smart young groom in his red and cream suit, and the little honey-coloured pony with the gleaming coat, whose hooves shone like black diamonds.

"Don't they look *sweet*," everyone agreed. "Three cheers for Jack and his pony."

But Jack's parents were in the crowd, and they had noticed the gleam in Patience's eye.

"There'll be trouble before long," said his father. "He's always been trouble, our Jack."

Everyone was cheering and waving. Jack's heart swelled with pride, as he led Patience over the bridge across the river.

Suddenly, Patience began to limp.

"Get along, you stupid beast!" hissed Jack, hitting her hard.

"Shame!" cried the crowd. "She's hurt. See what's wrong with her."

Jack did not dare disobey. He dropped the pony's reins, and walked round to examine her back leg.

The Queen's coach came to a sudden stop.

"What's the matter?" she cried, leaning out.

After that, everything happened very quickly. As Jack bent down to examine Patience's leg, she suddenly gave him one tremendous kick, a kick big enough for all the teasing and cruelty she had endured, a kick to send Jack flying over the parapet and right into the river!

The water wasn't very deep, so Jack was in no danger. But his red suit was ruined, and everyone in the crowd was laughing at the sight of him, sitting in the shallow water, covered in pondweed.

The crowd was so interested in Jack that they didn't notice the Queen standing by her favourite pony, looking thoughtful.

"Now why did you do that, Patience?" she asked. She knew her little pony would never hurt anyone, unless she was driven to do so. "That page will have to go," she said.

Now Jack sweeps the Palace driveway in a dirty old brown jacket and ragged trousers. And as Patience trots by, with the little Prince on her back, she sometimes cannot resist giving a little kick and a buck to show Jack that she has not forgotten him.

NOW YOU SEE ME, NOW YOU DON'T!

Marjorie Darke

I've got a white rosette hanging on my wall that isn't there. The rosette, I mean, not the wall! At least, it is there, but you can't see it. I bet you don't believe me, do you? Nobody does when I tell them. Feel the wallpaper for yourself. Go on, it's just under the horsey poster and next to my riding crop hanging on that nail. You're nearly there. A bit more to the left . . .

See!

I'll tell you about it.

The first thing you need to know is that I'm nuts about horses. You probably sussed that out already looking round my room. Posters, pony books, riding hat and boots, crop, the old bridle with the oil rag tucked in the snaffle, those bits of ribbon out of Topaz's tail. Mum says it's a tip, but I like having horsey things lying about. Makes me feel as if I've got a pony of my own. Which I haven't. Well – you can't stable a pony in a tower-block flat five floors up. There aren't any escalators and our lift is much too small. It would all be rather hopeless if it wasn't for Ellen.

Ellen's my cousin and Topaz is her pony. They live on a farm just outside our town. I go and stay with her quite often as we are both pony freaks, so get on together like knife and fork. Aunt Win's great too, and Uncle Sidney's not bad. Dustbin's the only blot. He's Ellen's little brother. His real name is Arnold and he's six. You'll understand the nickname when I tell you that as soon as I got through the farm front door that Gymkhana Saturday morning, he ran at me asking for sweets. I gave him a pony nut, though he still had a doorstep of toast in his hand. He gobbled it and was just asking for another when Ellen came roaring up from the kitchen. Specs slipping. Hedgehog hair. She always travels like a fire engine on the way to a warehouse blaze.

"Hi, Vi!" she said. (That's me – Violet.) "You're late. What happened?"

"Had a puncture," I explained. "Had to mend it."

"Hard cheese." Ellen had thrown off her slippers, seized a pair of old wellies and grabbed my arm, all without stopping. "Come on, there's masses to do. The tack's okay but Topaz is a wreck." She towed me through the kitchen, where Dustbin was polishing off the cat's milk and Aunt Win was ironing the newspaper, hardly giving me time to say "Hi!" before we were out and crossing the yard to the stable.

Topaz was a wreck. Enough mud on her to fill up a fish-pond. She seemed pleased to see me and began chewing my hair as soon as I got close to her. In her way she's as greedy as Dustbin.

Ellen handed me the dandy brush. "You start that side. I'll clean her hooves."

We slogged away, scraping and brushing, till Topaz shone like a copper kettle. Ellen stood back and admired her.

"Fantastic!"

"Super," I agreed.

"Just needs a rub of hoof oil and she'll win the Best Kept Horse prize easy. Get the bottle for me, Vi. It's on the shelf, I think." She had her back to me.

I rummaged amongst the junk and found a dusty bottle. Unscrewing the cap, I sniffed.

"Pooh, what a pong! Last week's kippered socks! You'll have to hold your nose." I held it out, grinning.

Ellen turned round. Well – I've never seen anyone's face change so much. Her eyes bulged. Her cheeks went rainbow. Her mouth opened and closed like that big carp they've got in a tank at our museum. She wasn't staring at me, she had her eyes glued on the bottle. I looked too.

It hung there, twitching ever so slightly. In my fright I almost dropped it.

There was no hand, no arm, no nothing!

"Holy cow!" I breathed, staring down. All I could see where the rest of me should have been was the dandy brush lying on the stable floor. "Where am I?"

Ellen came close and poked at me.

"Ow!" I said. "That nearly went in my eye."

She let out a big breath. "I was afraid I'd go through. You can't be a ghost, then. But what happened?"

"Dunno, do I?" I snapped. It wasn't her fault, of course, but I felt really weird and that made me cross. My skin tingled, which didn't seem right when it wasn't there. I was thinking terrible things about having to miss the Gymkhana and not being able to eat.

"Hey!" Ellen said suddenly. "I can see your knicker elastic and your wellies."

It was true. I was in such a flap I'd not noticed the pink circle stretched around my invisible middle, or my empty wellies. I took a step forward. The wellies moved like magic and the elastic wobbled, with the knot at the back bobbing like a cork at sea. I felt embarrassed, and wished now I'd remembered to sew it neatly when Mum told me.

Ellen had got over her first astonishment, and took the bottle off me. "It must be this. Let's see if I'm right."

Before I could stop her she'd tipped some oil on to a bit of old rag and was rubbing it over the dandy brush.

Nothing happened, except for smears of dirt on the rag and oil on the brush. I could see she was disappointed.

"What *exactly* did you do?" she asked.

"Sniffed it."

For one awful moment I thought she was going to do the same, then she saw her watch. "Crumbs, we're late. We haven't even changed yet!"

"Not much point in me changing," I said gloomily.

"Oh, don't be daft. Even if you don't bother with anything else you'll need your riding boots and hat for the clear-round jumping."

"How can I do clear-round jumping if I'm see-through?" I demanded.

But she wouldn't listen. "There's no time to argue. Come on!"

I didn't budge. "In wellies and knicker elastic . . . you have to be joking! Besides, if Aunt Win finds out what's happened she'll dose me with castor oil and tuck me up with a hot water bottle. You know how she is."

Ellen did. "Okay. You stay with Topaz. Shan't be long."

She wasn't and I changed quickly. It was very odd seeing my clothes appear and disappear all the time. For some reason all the things I put on vanished — except for the elastic. I did think of leaving my knickers off, but as Ellen said — what was the point when there was elastic under my hat as well?

The Gymkhana was in a field just beyond the next village. We had to hack there. Ellen on Topaz and me on my bike. Somehow we managed to get away without Aunt Win watching, though we had a near squeak when she came dashing out of the front door after Dustbin, who had nicked a bag of crisps and an apple turnover out of the picnic basket. I'd just got hold of my bike handlegrips. They disappeared immediately, like everything that touched me. I tried not to move – tried even not to breathe, hoping my elastics would blend with the wall and the flowerbed. Luckily she didn't seem to notice. But Dustbin did. I saw his eyes go big as dinner plates. That kid could see a gnat on a chimney-pot! He didn't get a chance to say anything though, because Aunt Win swept him up and went inside.

By this time Ellen and Topaz had come out of the yard and I made her ride behind me all the way to the gate and into the lane, in case anyone happened to glance out of a window. She kept giggling, and said the bike looked so silly with bites out of it where I was sitting and everything – just like something out of a Tom and Jerry cartoon she'd seen on telly, where Tom had been blatted and turned into a ghost.

"Oh, ha ha!" I said, rather sour. I mean, it isn't easy to see the funny side when it's you who's nothing but an empty space.

Ellen said: "Don't be such a drip. Think of all the things you'll be able to do."

I said: "What?"

And she said: "Go in for the competitions without paying."

I hadn't thought of this before, but it didn't seem much of a reward. How could I compete? A horse without a rider doesn't count. I pointed this out, but all she did was go on giggling. I felt so peeved that I pedalled like mad, shooting away from her round the corner . . . and came face to space with another cyclist.

The bloke on the bike swerved and his head nearly twisted back to front as we passed. There was a squeal of brakes and a scraping thud. I glanced back and saw him sitting halfway up the grass verge, underneath his bike. He looked dazed but okay, so I didn't stop, and in a minute Ellen caught up with me.

We were almost there and I was beginning to get really worried about what to do next. I'd been secretly hoping that the effect of smelling that yucky hoof oil would wear off, but so far I wasn't even cellophane thick. Another turn in the lane. Past the farm with the hayrick built like a house and . . .

There we were.

The Gymkhana was in full swing. Kids, ponies, parents, and all the people running it were seething over the field. A cotton wool voice was blaring instructions for the next competition through a loudspeaker. I saw some ponies and riders moving towards the starting place, past an ice cream van which stood near the hedge. The old excitement came boiling up and for a moment I forgot about being careful. Getting off my bike, I moved towards the gate where a tweedy woman was sitting at a card table collecting entrance money from the cars. She looked up, staring not at me, but at my bike, upright and alone, which wheeled towards her. Very slowly she blinked twice.

And then, as her eyelids opened up for the second time, I was back. Don't ask me to tell you how it happened, because I just don't know. One minute I was see-through as windows, the next tubby and solid as Christmas pud. It was just like switching on an electric light — that fast and easy.

I don't know whether the tweedy woman actually saw. What I do know is that she shook her head, then pulled one of those leather brandy flasks from her pocket and emptied it into the grass.

Ellen had got off Topaz and as we went in, she murmured: "Hard cheese!"

I knew she was still thinking about sneaking into the competitions without paying, but who cared about that? It was a pretty daft idea anyway.

The rest of the morning was great. Ellen competed in a sort of slalom, where you weave your pony in and out of some poles. She didn't win, but later she went in for the Musical Sacks and came first. Afterwards I had a go at the Egg and Spoon, but Topaz was bored or something and we were last. Then Aunt Win arrived with Dustbin and we had our picnic. All the time I stayed solid and for once didn't mind my podginess. It was so good to be able to see my knees and my feet and my sausagy hands. There was only one slight panic when we lost Dustbin. We found him in the ice cream van "helping" (that's his word not mine), which meant eating as much free ice cream as he could scrounge.

The afternoon was the high spot for me. Clear-round jumping. The course was arranged in another field leading off the first, and there were seven different sorts of jumps dotted about. I ought to explain that you can have as many tries as you like until you get a clear round. Everyone who does gets a white rosette. Ellen was one of the first to enter. She flew over the first four jumps. The fifth was a natural dip in the ground made into a ditch jump with a marker pole in front and behind. Topaz stopped dead in front of this and Ellen nearly went over her head. She took her back and tried again. This time Topaz jumped easily, but of course it had spoiled the clear round. Ellen was a bit cheesed, but she had the red rosette for the Musical Sacks, so didn't feel too bad. She could have had another go straight away, but she knew how much I wanted to try and said it was only fair I should have next turn. I thought that was ace – after all, Topaz is her pony.

We let Topaz have a rest while five other people had a go. Then it was my turn.

Topaz and I get on pretty well, considering she isn't my pony and I don't get that much practice. We hadn't done too well in the Egg and Spoon, but somehow as I settled into the saddle again I had this odd feeling that everything would go just right.

I queued up and paid my 40p, watching the girl

in front of me start off. Her pony knocked down two poles one after another, then missed the next jump, did three all right and finally tipped the girl into the brushwood fence.

I can do better than that, I thought, as the judge called: "Next one!"

We were off!

The first jump was a single low pole which we took with inches to spare. Next was another slightly higher pole with a couple of oil drums underneath. Then a tree trunk. Both those we sailed over. Bales of hay followed, and that's where the trouble started. Don't get me wrong, Topaz was jumping like a dream. Hay, the ditch where she'd stopped before, a third pole with boxes in front, finally the brushwood fence – she jumped the lot without even flicking anything with her heels. No . . . it was *me*! As we took off before the hay bales, I

vanished! Where I held the reins, where I sat on the saddle, where I touched Topaz with my legs — all that had vanished as well. The poor thing was as full of holes as a paper doily. By the time we touched down I was back. But I disappeared as we jumped the ditch. Again I came back, only to disappear for a third time. It was like being one of those Christmas fairy lights popping on and off every second. I felt dizzy, but there was nothing I could do except hang on and try remembering everything I'd learned about how to help your pony jump properly. I was too busy to see if the judges had noticed anything.

Of course they had!

As Topaz and I (see-through) came over the brushwood fence and landed (solid), the judge at the exit was as white as the rosette in her hand. I knew we'd had a clear round, so I rode up to collect it.

She backed away. Eyes like organ stops. Then she coughed and gasped: "Wait a minute!"

I waited.

The other judges came hurrying up, and as the exit judge joined them I could hear them arguing:

" . . . clear round. Yes, it was. Definitely."

"But over four of the jumps the pony had no rider. That can't mean a clear round."

"She couldn't have fallen off and remounted, surely?"

"She came over that last fence and *appeared*, I tell you. There's nothing in the rules to cover *that*!"

"But I was on Topaz all the time. Really I was," I burst out, unable to bear it any longer. It would be too mean if they refused to give Topaz and me the rosette we'd earned. "I only went see-through for a second. It happens sometimes."

Then an old bloke in a Sherlock Holmes hat, who seemed to be chief judge, said: "No, there is certainly no rule to cover instant vanishing, but I think no one can say it wasn't a clear round. You have won your rosette!" and he burst into a roar of laughter.

Then came the oddest thing of all. He insisted on tying the rosette round my sleeve, and as he did, it *vanished*! It was there all right. I could feel it. So could Ellen and Aunt Win when they tried. But it's never come back. Not from that day to this. Well — you know, don't you? You felt it. Sometimes I wonder if it did, whether I might vanish again. It hasn't happened so far and I get goose pimples when I think that way.

And my wellies and elastics staying solid all the time? Funny you should ask about that. I don't know the answer really. They were all rubbery things, of course. Dustbin thought of that. He's not a blot *all* the time. Sometimes he can be quite clever.

Ellen and I are still nuts about horses. We go to Gymkhanas too. But we never use hoof oil. To tell the truth we've never been able to find the bottle again. We have a sneaky feeling Dustbin knows something about that too, though he won't ever let on. But several of the farm cats have a funny way of just being there all of a sudden . . . and vanishing just as quick!

McGregor AND THE KELPY

A Scottish folktale retold by Dinah Starkey

There was a kelpy that haunted the shores of Loch Ness. It took the form of a black horse, but its coat had a greenish shine to it, like that dark seaweed you find on rocks. And it was wicked. It waited by the water's edge for passing travellers and drowned them deep in the loch.

Now the beast had the patience of Job, but strangers were few and far between and it must have grown tired of waiting about because one night Ian McGregor's daughter came running into their cottage with a face as white as cheese.

"Bolt the door!" she gasped. "It's after me!"

McGregor was a slow-moving sort of man, who didn't panic easily, but he got the bolt up like greased lightning because he could see the state she was in.

"Who?" he said. "What's the matter, lass?"

But the girl was sobbing so much she could hardly speak, and it was a long time before they could get the story out of her.

It seemed she'd been walking by the edge of the loch, looking for driftwood, when she saw a young man coming towards her.

"Oh, and he was handsome!" she said. "The bonniest man I ever saw. But strange looking, mind. And he knew my name. I thought that was funny because I knew fine I'd never seen him before. Well, we got talking and he was telling me all kinds of queer things about the loch – things I'd never dreamt of, though I've lived here all my life. And it was all so interesting that it was dinner time before we knew it, and he shared my bannock and cheese. Then he put his head in my lap and I began to comb his hair."

She gave a little gasp and then continued.

"But his hair was wet," she said. "Dripping wet, though I knew for a fact he hadn't been near the water since morning. He couldn't have been, you see, because he'd been talking to me. And the comb was full of sand and tiny pebbles. Then I saw he was watching me. He was laughing. Of course I knew fine what he was then, and why I'd never had a sight of him before. But I said 'You're all in a tangle, aren't you?' and carried on, as if I hadn't noticed. I didn't dare let him know I'd guessed for fear of what he'd do. I combed as softly and slowly as I could and bit by bit, his head felt heavier. His eyes were closing. But still I didn't stop. I went on till I was sure he was fast asleep and then I put his head down and I slipped away as quietly as ever I could. He didn't stir and for all I know he's asleep there still, but he knows my name and he knows where I live and he'll be after me, I know he will. Whatever am I going to do?"

At that she fell to crying again and McGregor stared into the fire.

"Whisht, lassie, it'll be all right," said her mother. "He can't get in here. You're safe now."

But Mairi wept on and would not be comforted, while her father glared into the fire. At last he said, "I'll see you safe, Mairi, and that's a promise. Elspeth, fetch my dirk. I'm off out and I'll not be back till late. You're to put rowan round the doors and windows so the beast can't get in. I'll teach it to play tricks with my daughter or my name's not Ian McGregor."

With that, he strode out into the twilight, dirk in hand. He went off down to the lake to search for the kelpy, but the dark was gathering and before long he began to doubt if he'd find it. He was just wondering whether to go home and try again next morning when before him, standing by the water, he saw a tall black horse. There was no one to be seen for miles around but the horse was saddled and bridled as if for riding and it watched him from the corner of its eye.

McGregor stood still and waited. The horse snorted and its bridle jingled in the still air. It looked ordinary enough and yet there was something not quite right about it. Its coat shone like seaweed and the set of its head was knowing.

It sidled closer, while McGregor eased his dirk from the sheath. It drew nearer and with it came the smell of lake water and a coldness. Then it was upon him, jostling him, forcing him back towards the loch, but it made no sound.

McGregor stumbled and almost lost his footing. The animal reared up, seizing its chance, and lashed at him with hooves as sharp as knives. Its ears were flat against its head and its eyes were wicked. He ducked, shielding himself as best he could and reached up to snatch at its bridle. As everyone knew, the power of a water horse lay in its bit. Without it, it was helpless.

But it was no easy task to grasp the bit, let alone cut it free. The kelpy forced him back and back, to the very edge of the loch, while McGregor hung on like grim death. He'd managed to slash through the leather on one side when it reared up over him, baring its teeth. The black water lay below him, deep and still and cold as death. He teetered, flung out a hand to save himself, and with the sudden strain the bit broke free. The horse screamed and flung itself into the loch.

McGregor sat down on a stone to get his breath back. He knew this wasn't the end by a long chalk. He thrust the bit deep in his pocket and waited for the next move. It was almost dark. He could just see the gleaming ripples on the water and presently, in the distance, a dark head broke the surface and came arrowing towards him. A young man pulled himself out of the water and came striding across the shore.

"Give it back," he said curtly.

McGregor shook his head.

"It's mine," said the young man. "You stole it."

Still McGregor made no reply and the young man took a step forward. His hair gleamed in the darkness.

"I'll give you gold," he said coaxingly. "I'll give you your heart's desire if you'll only let me have it."

"I don't want gold," said McGregor. "I want to see my family at peace and that they never will be while you have your bit."

"What will you do with it?"

"I'll keep it safe where you can never reach it."

The young man's fists clenched.

"Just you try!" he shouted. "Just try and get it home even. You'll never get it across the threshold for I'll be there, barring the way. And I'll have it back if it's the last thing I do!"

He wheeled, and was gone, running like a deer

across the heather. A patch of cloud covered the moon and when it cleared there was no sign of him. But a black horse thundered across the glen, heading for McGregor's croft.

It was some time later when McGregor reached home. Sure enough, he found the water horse waiting on the threshold, and he knew he hadn't a chance of getting past. Every window in the house was candlelit and the doors were decked with rowan. He could see his wife and daughter peering anxiously through the glass but the water horse pawed the ground and he was on the outside, in the dark.

Mairi cried, "Give him the bit, Father. He says he won't move until you do."

But McGregor gripped it all the tighter and began inching round to slip in behind the water horse. He had his hand on the door-knob when it struck at him so sharply that he gasped. Its ears flattened and it drove him backwards. His wife had got the big iron cooking pot and she hurled it at the kelpy to try and drive it away. But though the blow fell square and the beast squealed with pain and fury it would not give way. It stood four square in front of the door and McGregor could see no way of getting by.

He looked at the house, protected by rowan, and he knew that if he could only get the bit inside he'd be safe. And suddenly he knew how to do it.

"Elspeth!" he cried. "Catch hold!"

The bit flew up to her window, glittering in its flight. The horse reared in a vain attempt to seize it and Elspeth's hands stretched out, fumbled for a second, and then had it safe.

"Be off!" she shouted. "The bit's out of your reach now and you must do as I say."

She waved it in triumph and the water horse was still, watching. Suddenly it tossed its mane and galloped away, running like the wind. It never stopped till it reached the loch and that was the last the McGregors saw of it. There was no more trouble for them after that, nor for anyone else. And there never has been, to this very day.

A HAT
FOR CRUMPET

Barbee Oliver Carleton

Crumpet was a big friendly trolley-horse. "Maybe I shouldn't say so," declared Crumpet. "But I suppose I'm the biggest, friendliest trolley-horse in all New York!"

Crumpet was right. Wherever she went, clippity clop, East Side, West Side, all around the town, people looked twice at Crumpet. Even the Mayor.

"And I suppose," thought Crumpet happily, "that Billy Bailey is the smartest-looking driver anywhere in the world."

Sure enough. Bill Bailey sat high and handsome on the driver's seat behind Crumpet. He tipped his hat to everyone as smartly as you please.

"Without a doubt," went on Crumpet, looking over her shoulder, "our trolley is the prettiest little trolley you ever did see."

And it was, indeed. Golden squiggles all over the sides. Scallops on the top. "And the nicest people in New York," Crumpet decided, "sitting on the red plush seats." The mothers in their neat straw hats. The fathers in their bowler hats. The dearest and the cleanest children in the world. And ONE fine spring morning, the Mayor himself!

"Top of the morning, Bill Bailey!" he boomed. "And what's an elegant horse like Crumpet doing without a hat? Every trolley-horse in New York has a hat!"

Elegant! The Mayor called her ELEGANT! Pointing her toes, Crumpet trotted off so smartly that all the nice passengers held on to their hats to avoid losing them.

"Sure, Your Honour," laughed Bill Bailey. "I'll get her a hat for Easter."

All the way down Fifth Avenue, Crumpet peered into the hat shops. She wondered which hat Bill Bailey would buy. "Maybe," she thought, "it will be that sailor hat with the ribbons down the back. Or maybe," whispered Crumpet, "one of

those wide, beautiful, elegant hats with roses around the brim!" At the very thought, Crumpet did a two-step all the way to City Hall.

That night Crumpet dreamed about hats — all sorts of hats. And every one of them was beautiful and fancy.

Next morning, in came Bill Bailey with Crumpet's breakfast. And something else.

"Here you are, Crumpet!" he sang. "Here's the comfiest, droopiest old hat anywhere in town! Found it on the dump!" And Bill Bailey, because he loved Crumpet, carefully cut two large holes for Crumpet's ears. He put the hat on Crumpet's head. "Very smart!" said Bill Bailey. Then off they started up the Avenue.

Poor Crumpet. Maybe, if she tiptoed very softly . . . and hung her head very low . . . maybe nobody would notice . . .

"WHAT'S THE MATTER WITH CRUMPET?" everybody asked in surprise.

"I wish I knew," worried Bill Bailey.

"I hate to say it," said the Mayor, "but an elegant trolley like this trolley needs an elegant horse to pull it."

All the nice passengers stared at Crumpet, dragging her feet up ahead. "What's the matter with Crumpet?" they asked one another.

But the children, who loved Crumpet very much, knew exactly what was the matter. They whispered to Bill Bailey. Bill Bailey said, "Well, what do you know!" Then, "Maybe you're right!" And finally, "A splendid idea!"

Crumpet, with her head hanging down by her knees and the old hat drooping over her eyes, heard the whispers. Then she heard the secret clinking of lots of coins. And then, right in front of a hat shop, she heard the CLANG-CLANG of the trolley-bell. Crumpet stopped. Some passengers got off. Crumpet's heart was so heavy that she didn't even wonder what Bill Bailey was waiting for. She squeezed her eyes tight shut to hold back the tears.

Then a voice said softly, "Crumpet, this is for you."

Crumpet lifted her head. There beside her were the children, taking something out of a box. A something that was wide and beautiful and elegant! It was blooming with roses and streaming with streamers! Off came the comfy old hat. On went the beautiful new one. Gently, the children tied the streamers under Crumpet's chin.

"Happy Easter, Crumpet!" they smiled. Then they hopped back on to the trolley.

CLANG–CLANG–CLANG! went the bell. Up came Crumpet's head in the elegant hat. She pointed her toes daintily. Then, with her nose held high and her roses bobbing and her streamers flying, off down the avenue she trotted.

All the way along the route, Crumpet sang to herself: "CLIPPITY-CLOP! TWIDDLE-DEE-DEE! THIS IS JUST THE HAT FOR A HORSE LIKE ME!"

UNICORN

Peter Dickinson

Rhiannon was an orphan and lived with her grandmother in a village at the edge of the forest. She was one of Sir Brangwyn's orphans, as they called them in those parts – that is to say her parents were alive but her father was imprisoned in the dungeons of Castle Grim and her mother worked in the castle kitchens to earn money to pay for his food. He had done nothing wrong, but Sir Brangwyn had accused him of stealing deer. Sir Brangwyn liked to have the best men from all the villages in his dungeons, so that the other villagers would stay quiet and good, and hardly dare murmur when he taxed them of every farthing they had. Everyone knew that Rhiannon's father was innocent. If he had really been stealing deer Sir Brangwyn would have hanged him from the nearest tree.

Rhiannon was not allowed to go with her parents to the castle. Sir Brangwyn made a point of leaving the children behind, to remind the other villagers to be good. So she stayed in the village and did her share of the work. Everybody in the village had to work or starve, and since Rhiannon was only nine her job was to hunt in the forest for truffles.

The forest was enormous – nobody knew how big, or what lay deep inside it. Some said that strange beasts laired there, dragons and unicorns and basilisks, which could turn you to stone by looking at you. Others said all that had happened in the old days, and the strange beasts were gone, so now there were only ordinary animals such as boars and deer and wolves and bears. Sometimes Sir Brangwyn would come and hunt these. Hunting was the one thing he cared about in all the world.

Rhiannon never went deep into the forest. She always stayed where she could see the edge. Truffles are hard to find. They are a leathery black fungus which grows underground on the roots of certain trees, and for those who like rich food (as Sir Brangwyn did) they add a particularly delicious taste and smell. Rhiannon always hoped that one day she would find so many truffles that Sir Brangwyn would send her parents home as a reward, but it did not happen. She seldom found more than a few, and sometimes she would dig in forty places and find none.

Exactly a year after the soldiers had come to take her father away, Rhiannon went off to the forest as usual. But not at all as usual, she was followed back that evening by a small white horse, no more than a foal, pure silvery white with a silky mane and tail.

The villagers were amazed.

"It must have escaped from some lord's stable," they said, and they tried to catch it, thinking there would be a reward. But before they came anywhere near, away it darted, glimmering across the meadows and into the dark woods. Then they found, to their further amazement, that Rhiannon's basket was full of truffles.

"My little horse showed me where to dig," she said.

This seemed very good news. Sir Brangwyn's tax-clerk would be coming to the village in a few days' time. Truffles were rare and expensive. Perhaps they could pay all their taxes in truffles, and that would mean they would have a little food to spare for themselves this year. So next morning a dozen men and women went up with Rhiannon to the forest, hoping the little horse would come and show them where to dig. But they saw no sign of it and they found nothing for themselves, so at noon they went back to their own tasks, leaving Rhiannon behind. Again that evening the white horse came glimmering behind her almost to the edge of the village, then dashed away. And again Rhiannon's basket was full of truffles.

So it went on every day until the tax-clerk came, and the headman brought him a whole sackload of truffles to pay the taxes. This clerk was a monk, who could read and write. He knew things which ordinary people did not know. When he asked how it happened that the village had so many truffles to send, the headman told him. The headman was a simple fellow. (Sir Brangwyn saw to it that the clever ones were in his dungeons.)

That evening the clerk sent for a huntsman and told him what he wanted, and next night the huntsman came back and told what he had seen. He had followed Rhiannon up to the forest, taking care to keep out of sight, and at the forest edge a little white horse had come cavorting out and kissed Rhiannon on the forehead, and then she had followed it in under the trees where it had run to and fro, sniffling and snuffling like a dog, and every now and then it would stop and paw with its hoof on the ground, and Rhiannon would dig there and find truffles. The horse was obviously extremely shy of anyone but Rhiannon and kept looking nervously around, so the huntsman had not been able to come close, but then, when Rhiannon's basket was full, she had sat down with her back against a tree and the horse had knelt by her side and put its head in her lap and gazed into her eyes and she had sung to it. The little horse had been so entranced that it seemed to forget all danger, and the huntsman had been able to creep close enough to see it well.

"And sure, it's a very fine wee beast, your honour," he said to the clerk. "What it'll be doing in these woods I can't be guessing. And it's never seen bit or bridle, I'll be bound, never seen stall nor stable. As for the colour of its coat, it is whiter than snow, not a touch nor fleck of grey nor of yellow in it. Only one thing . . . "

"Yes?" whispered the clerk, as though he knew what was coming.

"The pity of it is the animal's face, for it's misshapen. It has this lump, or growth as it might be, big as my bent thumb between the eyes."

"Ah," said the clerk.

Next morning he left his tax-gathering and hurried to Castle Grim to tell Sir Brangwyn there was a unicorn in the woods.

The great hall of Castle Grim was hung with the trophies of Sir Brangwyn's hunting. Deer and hare, boar and badger, wolf and fox, heron and dove, he had ridden it down or dug it up or hawked it out of the air. But he had never hunted unicorn. Before the clerk had finished his message Sir Brangwyn was on his feet and bellowing for his huntsmen and his grooms, and in an hour he was on the road with a dozen expert trackers and twenty couple of hounds.

The people of Rhiannon's village were glad to see him come. Sometimes when a village had shown him good sport he had let the people off their taxes for a whole year. So here they were

eager to help. They beat the woods, they dug traps where they were told, they set watch, but it was all no use. Sir Brangwyn's clever hounds bayed to and fro and found nothing. His trackers found the prints of an unshod foal all over the truffle-grounds, but lost the trail among the trees.

After three days of this Sir Brangwyn's temper soured, and the villagers began to be anxious. Then the tax-clerk explained what Sir Brangwyn had been too impatient to hear before, that the only way to hunt a unicorn is to send a maiden alone into the woods, and the unicorn will come to her and lay its head in her lap and be so enraptured by her singing that he will not see the huntsmen coming.

Sir Brangwyn had not brought any maidens with him, but the village headman told him about Rhiannon. All that night the villagers toiled by torchlight, cutting brushwood and building a great bank of it by the truffle-grounds, high enough to hide a mounted man. In the morning they took Rhiannon up to the forest. When they told her what she had to do she tried to say no, but by this time Sir Brangwyn had learnt where her parents were, and he explained to her what would happen to them if she refused. So she went into the forest and sat down, weeping, in her usual place, while Sir Brangwyn waited hidden behind the bank of brushwood.

For a long while everything was still.

Then, suddenly, there was a glimmering deep in the dark wood and the unicorn came delicately out, looking this way and that, hesitating, sniffing the wind. When it was sure all was safe it cavorted up to Rhiannon and kissed her on the forehead and knelt by her side with its head on her lap, gazing up into her eyes, puzzled why she did not sing. Sir Brangwyn broke from his hide, spurring the sides of his horse till the blood runnelled. The nearing hooves drubbed like thunder.

Then Rhiannon could bear it no more. She jumped to her feet with her arms round the unicorn's neck, dragging it up, and turned its head so that it could see Sir Brangwyn coming.

At once it reared away, giving Rhiannon no time to loose her hold. The movement twitched her sideways and up so that she was lying along the unicorn's back with her arms round its neck and the unicorn was darting away under the trees with Sir Brangwyn hallooing behind, his spear poised for the kill.

The hoofbeats dwindled into the forest, into

silence. Then huntsmen and villagers, waiting out of sight beyond the forest, heard a voice like the snarl of trumpets, a man's shout and a crash. Then silence once more.

The trackers followed the hoofprints deep into the dark wood. They found Sir Brangwyn's body under an oak tree, pierced through from side to side. His horse they caught wandering close by.

Rhiannon came out of the forest at sunset. What had she seen and heard? What fiery eye, what silvery mane? What challenge and what charge? She would not say.

Only when her mother and father came home, set free by Sir Brangwyn's heir, she told them something. They had taken her to her bed and were standing looking down at her, full of their happiness in being all three together again, and home, when she whispered four words.

"Unicorns have parents too."

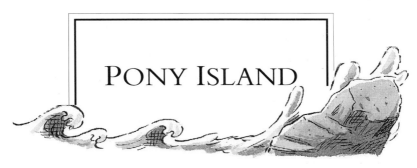

PONY ISLAND

Ann Wigley

Jenny's grandmother lived in a little fishing village called Wrack, that stood by itself on a wild, windy, empty shore. Grandmother's cottage looked out over the tussocky sand dunes, the long beach and the restless sea that beat around Pony Island. Every summer, Jenny and her parents went to stay for a holiday with her.

Jenny knew everyone in Wrack, but her special friends were the fishermen. She loved to sit on the shingle above the tideline and listen, while the fishermen mended their nets and told her wonderful stories of the sea. Always respect the sea, the fishermen warned Jenny. It can be calm and friendly one minute, then wild and treacherous the next. Storms can blow up out of nowhere, especially in the dangerous waters around Pony Island.

Pony Island, in the middle of Wrack Bay, was surrounded by sea at high tide but, when the tide went out, you could walk to the island across a sandy causeway. You would have to be quick about it, though, because soon the water would come slipping and sliding back to trap the unwary walker.

Sometimes, on a clear, sunny day, the island appeared to be very close, and Jenny could see the grass and bushes bending in the breeze and brown shapes dotted across the island. On other days, the island looked very far away and was almost lost in sea haze and flying spray, and the brown shapes seemed to move mysteriously in the shifting mist. Jenny was sure that the brown shapes were ponies living wild on the island, and she longed to see them.

"Don't be silly, Jenny. Nobody ever goes to Pony Island," Grandmother said.

"There is nothing to see there that is worth the risk of crossing the causeway," the fishermen agreed.

Jenny was disappointed, but at least she had Ned the donkey to ride. Ned, who lived in a paddock behind Grandmother's cottage, had long, grey, furry ears; a brown, whiskery muzzle, and the dark donkey cross on his back. Jenny was allowed to ride Ned whenever she liked. Grandmother knew that the gentle donkey could be trusted always to bring Jenny safely home again.

One afternoon, when Jenny rode Ned to the beach, she saw that the tide was a long, long way out. In the clear, sunlit air, Pony Island looked almost close enough to touch. The causeway was wide and dry – more than twice as wide as the village street and, surely, just as safe. Jenny could not resist the temptation to visit the wild ponies. It would not take Ned long to trot across the causeway, and they would be back even before the tide turned.

It took much longer than Jenny expected to cross the hard, rippled sand of the causeway. The afternoon wore on and turned overcast and chilly, but all the time those brown shapes were growing nearer and clearer, and Jenny's excitement mounted. She was certain, now, that they were ponies.

The causeway ended in a slope of shingle that clattered behind Ned as he climbed. It was windy on the island, and the shadows of gathering storm clouds raced ahead of Jenny and her donkey. There were no tracks through the tall, tangled grasses and scrubby bushes, and the going was difficult. Eventually, Ned puffed to a halt and refused to go any further.

Jenny stood in her stirrups and peered ahead. There they were at last! The brown shapes were spread out across the island and clear to see, but Jenny almost cried aloud with the bitterness of her disappointment. The brown shapes were not ponies. They were nothing like ponies. They were just rocks; huge outcrops of bare, wind-scoured

rock. Sadly, Jenny turned Ned round and urged him back to the shore.

When they got there, Jenny gasped with alarm. At this end the causeway was now no more than a narrow path with choppy, grey water cresting into angry wavelets on either side. Suddenly frightened, Jenny wanted to get home as quickly as possible, but home looked a very long way away. A sea-fret hazed the distance, and Jenny could barely see the beach and village of Wrack. Her heels pummelled Ned's sides in desperation, and the donkey flung himself down the shingle to the sand.

"Faster, Ned, faster," Jenny urged. She knew that they had only a little time before the dry path home vanished under the sea. Ned was galloping as if he sensed that they must run for their lives. His little un-shod donkey feet threw up spurts of sand behind him, and left hoof prints that quickly filled with water.

Closing in on either side of the racing donkey, sinister ripples reached to reclaim the causeway. Then a wave bigger than the rest swirled around Ned's legs. He stopped dead and spun round, to flee back to the island, but already the sea had closed behind him. Ned threw up his head and shrieked a harsh, despairing donkey bray of terror.

Their only hope was to race the in-coming tide. The way ahead was still dry, but getting narrower all the time. Every second must count because,

once even a little water covered the causeway, they
might miss the safe path and
gallop helplessly into the
deep sea. But Ned was para-
lyzed by fear. He refused to
move even a step and, once
again, he brayed his despair.

Then, an answering call
came from Pony Island. The
neigh of a horse was carried on
the wind, and the voice of the
horse was joined by others, snorting
and whinnying. Jenny turned in her saddle and saw
them coming, a herd of ponies, bay and black, grey
and chestnut, thundering across the island. The
herd crashed down the shingle beach and plunged
into the sea. Within seconds, the ponies of Pony
Island were all around Jenny and her donkey.

Jenny could smell the clean, sweet scent of the
ponies. She could feel the warmth of their breath
on her hands and face. She could see their manes
and tails whipping in the wind. She could look
into their dark, kind eyes and reach out to touch
their damp coats, as they pressed on either side of
Ned and forced him to go along with them.

The herd was galloping towards the far shore,
and Ned had no choice but to gallop with it. The
water was by now deep on the causeway, but the

ponies seemed to know the safe path by instinct. Their plunging hooves threw up a cascade of spray that drenched Jenny to the skin, but she just threw back her head and laughed aloud with relief and happiness. Jenny knew that she was quite safe now, in the care of the wise, wild ponies.

The glory of that breathtaking ride through wind and water, with the surging bodies and flying manes of the ponies all around her, was the most amazing experience of Jenny's life. The memory of it, she knew, would stay with her for ever. Then, all too soon, it was over.

The splash and suck of the ponies' feet, galloping in water, changed to the pounding thud of hooves on dry sand. They had reached the end of the causeway ahead of the rising tide, and the herd swept on up the beach towards the village. Ned must have put on an extra turn of speed, Jenny thought, because the wild ponies fell behind him and he cantered alone through the sand dunes.

A crowd of people, with worried faces and anxious voices, ran to meet Jenny. She was swept from her saddle and hugged by her sobbing mother, then hugged and hugged again by her frightened father. Her grandmother took the reins of the exhausted, trembling donkey, and all the fishermen were talking at once.

"Jenny, Jenny, why did you do such a silly thing?" her mother asked.

"I wanted to see the ponies on Pony Island," Jenny told her.

"But there are no ponies on the island," her grandmother said.

"Yes, there are! There is a whole herd of them." Jenny looked back at the beach, expecting to see the ponies that had galloped the causeway beside her. The beach was empty. The ponies had gone, and they had left not even a hoofprint in the sand.

"You must all have seen the ponies," Jenny insisted. "They saved my life because Ned was too frightened to go on until they made him."

"No, dear, we didn't see any ponies," Grandmother said, "just you and Ned racing the tide."

"And you must never do it again," Jenny's father told her, severely. "There is nothing to see on the island, and there are certainly no ponies living there."

"There were once," one of the fishermen

suddenly remembered. "That was how Pony Island got its name. There was a herd living there wild, long ago, before the great storm and the terrible high sea that swept right over the island. All the ponies were drowned. Some people say that the ponies haunt the island still."

The fishermen, walking back to the village, laughed at the absurdity of such a story. Jenny, too, was laughing, but she was laughing because she had a wonderful secret. No matter what anyone else said, Jenny knew that she had seen the beautiful, free ponies of Pony Island.

THE HORSE
OF FIRE AND
THUNDER

Maggie Pearson

"Hush, child!" whispered the King, rocking his baby son in his arms. "Don't cry. For you are a prince and one day you will be King of All the Russias."

Still little Prince Ivan went on crying.

"Hush, child! And I will get you a crown to wear and clothes of rainbow-coloured silk and a singing bird in a golden cage."

But still the baby cried.

"Hush, child! And you shall have youth without ageing and life without death."

Then the little Prince stopped crying and fell asleep.

In time the King forgot his promise, but Prince Ivan remembered it, even though he had been just a baby when it was made. When the King asked him what he wanted for his sixteenth birthday, Prince Ivan said, "I want the thing you promised me when I was little. Youth without ageing and life without death."

The King shook his head. "Did I promise that? That is a gift even a king cannot give."

"Then," said Prince Ivan, "give me a horse from your stable and I will go and find it for myself."

"Very well," the King agreed. A promise is a promise, after all. Even kings – kings most of all – should keep their promises. He told Prince Ivan to choose any horse he wanted.

Prince Ivan wandered through the royal stables, but no horse seemed quite right for such a journey. At last he came to the very end stall, where an ancient creature lay, all skin and bone.

"What horse is that?" asked the Prince.

The King sighed. "In your grandfather's time, they called him the Horse of Fire and Thunder. But the fire in him is ashes now and his thunder is no more than a whisper on the wind."

Prince Ivan bent his head and heard the horse's voice, so soft that only he could hear it: "Take me and care for me and I will be the Horse of Fire and Thunder again. I will carry you wherever you choose to go, even to the Land of the Ever-Young, where there is youth without ageing and life without death."

"This is the horse for me," Prince Ivan said, and he took it and looked after it until it was strong again.

Then the two of them set out together, through the wide world, searching for the Land of the Ever-Young.

They travelled across a wide plain, scattered with dead men's bones. Over the high mountains, bleak and cold. Through a land all blackened and scorched by fire.

They came at last to a deep, dark forest, where the sun never shone. The Horse of Fire and Thunder said: "Beyond this forest lies the Land of the Ever-Young. But we dare not go through it, for fear of the wild things that live there. I must leap over it at a single bound."

For three days the Horse of Fire and Thunder rested, gathering his strength.

On the
evening of the
third day, with
Prince Ivan on his
back, the horse leapt up, up into the sky. Below
them in the forest, the wild things – creatures of
nightmare, slimy shape-shifters, shadows without
eyes, and dead men walking with their heads on
back-to-front – screamed and clutched at the air.

But in the sunset sky ahead, Prince Ivan could
see a palace forming out of the shifting clouds and
people, beautiful people, holding out their arms to
welcome him.

"Prince Ivan!"

"What a long time you have been!"

"We have been waiting for you for sixteen years."

There is no way of counting how long he stayed in the Land of the Ever-Young. On every tree, spring blossoms clustered all year round, alongside the autumn fruits. Every day was full of sunshine and happiness, music and laughter, and games to play. There was no pain, no anger, no illness, no death.

Time passed.

Prince Ivan began to miss his home and the people he loved. "I must go back," he said. "Just to see them. Just to let them know I'm safe."

"Things have changed," said the horse. "You've been here longer than you think. They will have forgotten you by now."

"All the more reason to go," said Prince Ivan.

"Very well. But once we leave the Land of the Ever-Young, you must stay on my back. If you set even one foot upon the ground, you can never return here again."

So they set off, flying once more over the forest where the wild things were, but finding it silent now. They crossed the land which had been black and scorched by fire, but found it covered with fields of waving corn. The mountains, once so bleak and cold, were no more than a range of gentle hills. The plain that had been scattered with dead men's bones was covered with grass and running streams, and herds of sheep were quietly grazing.

When at last they came to the place where Prince Ivan's father's palace had been, they found no sign of it at all.

"Where is the palace of the King?" he asked.

"The King?" they said. "We have no king. Which king do you mean? Oh, *that* king! The

father of Prince Ivan, who rode away on the Horse of Fire and Thunder and never came back. That was more than a thousand years ago!"

They took him to a graveyard of low, grassy mounds, with headstones so worn he couldn't read the names. They showed him the tomb, all covered with moss and roses, where the old King lay.

Prince Ivan's eyes filled with tears. Forgetting the horse's warning, he flung himself from its back and knelt down among the graves.

But once on his knees, there was no getting up again. As soon as his foot touched the ground, he began to grow older. A thousand years older. His flesh withered and his bones crumbled into dust and mingled with the dust of the people he had loved.

The Horse of Fire and Thunder galloped away, and as far as I know he's living still, in the Land of the Ever-Young.

ROCKING-HORSE LAND

Laurence Housman

Little Prince Freedling woke up with a jump, and sprang out of bed into the sunshine. He was five years old that morning, by all the clocks and calendars in the kingdom; and the day was going to be beautiful. Every golden minute was precious. He was dressed and out of the room before the attendants knew that he was awake.

In the antechamber stood piles on piles of glittering presents; when he walked among them they came up to the measure of his waist. His fairy godmother had sent him a toy with the most humorous effect. It was labelled, "Break me and I shall turn into something else." So every time he broke it he got a new toy more beautiful than the last. It began by being a hoop, and from that it ran on, while the Prince broke it incessantly for the space of one hour, during which it became by turn a top, a Noah's ark, a skipping-rope, a man-of-war, a box of bricks, a picture puzzle, a pair of stilts, a drum, a trumpet, a kaleidoscope, a steam engine, and nine hundred and fifty other things exactly. Then he began to grow discontented, because it would never turn into the same thing again; and after having broken the man-of-war he wanted to get it back again. Also he wanted to see if the steam engine would go inside the Noah's ark; but the toy would never be two things at the same time either. This was very unsatisfactory. He thought his fairy godmother ought to have sent him two toys, out of which he could make combinations.

At last he broke it once more, and it turned into a kite; and while he was flying the kite he broke the string, and the kite went sailing away up into the nasty blue sky, and was never heard of again.

Then Prince Freedling sat down and howled at his fairy godmother; what a dissembling lot fairy godmothers were, to be sure! They were always setting traps to make their godchildren unhappy. Nevertheless, when told to, he took up his pen and wrote her a nice little note, full of bad spelling and tarradiddles, to say what a happy birthday he was spending in breaking up the beautiful toy she had sent him.

Then he went to look at the rest of the presents, and found it quite refreshing to break a few that did not send him giddy by turning into anything else.

Suddenly his eyes became fixed with delight; alone, right at the end of the room, stood a great black rocking-horse. The saddle and bridle were hung with tiny gold bells and balls of coral; and the horse's tail and mane flowed till they almost touched the ground.

The Prince scampered across the room, and threw his arms around the beautiful creature's neck. All its bells jingled as the head swayed gracefully down; and the Prince kissed it between the eyes. Great eyes they were, the colour of fire, so wonderfully bright, it seemed they must be really alive, only they did not move, but gazed continually with a set stare at the tapestry hung walls on which were figures of armed knights riding to battle.

So Prince Freedling mounted the back of his rocking-horse and all day long he rode and shouted to the figures of the armed knights, challenging them to fight, or leading them against the enemy.

At length, when it came to be bedtime, weary of so much glory, he was lifted down from the saddle and carried away to bed.

In his sleep Freedling still felt his black rocking-horse swinging to and fro under him, and heard the melodious chime of its bells, and, in the land of dreams, saw a great country open before him, full of the sound of the battle-cry and the hunting-horn calling him to strange perils and triumphs.

In the middle of the night he grew softly awake, and his heart was full of love for his black rocking-horse. He crept gently out of bed: he would go and look at it where it was standing so grand and still in the next room, to make sure it was all safe and not afraid of being by itself in the dark night. Parting the door-hangings he passed through into the wide hollow chamber beyond, all littered about with toys.

The moon was shining in through the window, making a square cistern of light upon the floor. And then, all at once, he saw that the rocking-horse had moved from the place where he had left it! It had crossed the room, and was standing close to the window, with its head toward the night, as though watching the movement of the clouds and the trees swaying in the wind.

The Prince could not understand how it had been moved so; he was a little bit afraid, and stealing timidly across, he took hold of the bridle to comfort himself with the jangle of its bells. As he came close, and looked up into the dark solemn face, he saw that the eyes were full of tears, and reaching up felt one fall warm against his hand.

"Why do you weep, my Beautiful?" said the Prince.

The rocking-horse answered, "I weep because I am a prisoner, and not free. Open the window, Master, and let me go!"

"But if I let you go I shall lose you," said the Prince. "Cannot you be happy here with me?"

"Let me go," said the horse, "for my brothers call me out of Rocking-Horse Land; I hear my mare whinnying to her foals; and they all cry, seeking me through the ups and hollows of my native fastnesses! Sweet Master, let me go this night, and I will return to you when it is day!"

Then Freedling said, "How shall I know that you will return: and what name shall I call you by?"

And the rocking-horse answered, "My name is Rollonde. Search my mane till you find in it a white hair; draw it out and wind it upon one of your fingers; and so long as you have it so wound you are my master; and wherever I am I must return at your bidding."

So the Prince drew down the rocking-horse's

head, and searching the mane, he found the white hair, and wound it upon his finger and tied it. Then he kissed Rollonde between the eyes, saying, "Go, Rollonde, since I love you, and wish you to be happy; only return to me when it is day!" And so saying, he threw open the window to the stir of the night.

Then the rocking-horse lifted his dark head and neighed aloud for joy, and swaying forward with a mighty circling motion rose full into the air, and sprang out into the free world before him.

Freedling watched how with plunge and curve he went over the bowed trees; and again he neighed into the darkness of the night, then swifter than wind he disappeared in the distance. And faintly from far away came a sound of the neighing of many horses answering him.

Then the Prince closed the window and crept back to bed: and all night long he dreamed strange dreams of Rocking-Horse Land. There he saw smooth hills and valleys that rose and sank without a stone or a tree to disturb the steel-like polish of their surface, slippery as glass, and driven over by a strong wind; and over them, with a sound like the humming of bees, flew the rocking-horses. Up and down, up and down, with bright manes streaming like coloured fires, and feet motionless behind and before, went the swift pendulum of their flight. Their long bodies bowed and rose; their heads worked to give impetus to their going; they cried, neighing to each other over hill and valley, "Which of us shall be first? Which of us shall be first?" After them the mares with their tall foals came spinning to watch, crying also among themselves, "Ah! which shall be first?"

"Rollonde, Rollonde is first!" shouted the Prince, clapping his hands as they reached the goal; and at that, all at once, he woke and saw it was broad day. Then he ran and threw open the window, and holding out the finger that carried the white hair, cried, "Rollonde, Rollonde, come back, Rollonde!"

Far away he heard an answering sound; and in another moment there came the great rocking-horse himself, dipping and dancing over the hills. He crossed the woods and cleared the

palace wall at a bound, and floating in through the window, dropped to rest at Prince Freedling's side, rocking gently to and fro as though panting from the strain of his long flight.

"Now are you happy?" asked the Prince as he caressed him.

"Ah! sweet Prince," said Rollonde. "Ah, kind Master!" And then he said no more, but became the still staring rocking-horse of the day before, with fixed eyes and rigid limbs, which could do nothing but rock up and down with a jangling of sweet bells so long as the Prince rode him.

That night Freedling came again when all was still in the palace; and now as before Rollonde had moved from his place and was standing with his head against the window waiting to be let out. "Ah, dear Master," he said, so soon as he saw the Prince coming, "let me go this night also, and surely I will return with day."

So again the Prince opened the window, and watched him disappear, and heard from far away the neighing of the horses in Rocking-Horse Land calling to him. And in the morning with the white hair round his finger he called "Rollonde, Rollonde!" and Rollonde neighed and came back to him, dipping and dancing over the hills.

Now this same thing happened every night; and every morning the horse kissed Freedling, saying, "Ah! dear Prince and kind Master," and became stock still once more.

So a year went by, till one morning Freedling woke up to find it was his sixth birthday. And as six is to five, so were the presents he received on his sixth birthday for magnificence and multitude to the presents he had received the year before. His fairy godmother had sent him a bird, a real live bird; but when he pulled its tail it became a lizard, and when he pulled the lizard's tail it became a mouse, and when he pulled the mouse's tail it became a cat. Then he did very much want to see if the cat would eat the mouse, and not being able to have them both he got rather vexed with his fairy godmother. However, he pulled the cat's tail and the cat became a dog, and when he pulled the dog's tail the dog became a goat; and so it went on till he got to a cow. And he pulled the cow's tail and it became a camel, and he pulled the camel's tail and it became an elephant, and still not being contented, he pulled the elephant's tail and it became a guinea-pig. Now a guinea-pig has no tail to pull, so it remained a guinea-pig, while Prince

Freedling sat down and howled at his fairy godmother.

But the best of all his presents was the one given to him by the King, his father. It was a most beautiful horse, for, said the King, "You are now old enough to learn to ride."

So Freedling was put upon the horse's back and from having ridden so long upon his rocking-horse he learned to ride perfectly in a single day, and was declared by all the courtiers to be the most perfect equestrian that was ever seen.

Now these praises and the pleasure of riding a real horse so occupied his thoughts that that night he forgot all about Rollonde, and falling fast asleep dreamed of nothing but real horses and horsemen going to battle. And so it was the next night too.

But the night after that, just as he was falling asleep, he heard someone sobbing by his bed, and a voice saying, "Ah! dear Prince and kind Master, let me go for my heart breaks for a sight of my native land." And there stood his poor rocking-horse Rollonde, with tears falling out of his beautiful eyes on to the white coverlet.

Then the Prince, full of shame at having forgotten his friend, sprang up and threw his arms round his neck saying, "Be of good cheer, Rollonde, for now surely I will let thee go!" and he ran to the window and opened it for the horse to go through. "Ah, dear Prince and kind Master!" said Rollonde. Then he lifted his head and neighed so that the whole palace shook, and swaying forward till his head almost touched the ground, he sprang out into the night and away towards Rocking-Horse Land.

Then Prince Freedling, standing by the window, thoughtfully unloosed the white hair from his finger, and let it float away into the darkness, out of sight of his eye or reach of his hand.

"Goodbye, Rollonde," he murmured softly, "brave Rollonde, my own good Rollonde! Go and be happy in your own land, since I, your master, was forgetting to be kind to you." And far away he heard the neighing of horses in Rocking-Horse Land.

Many years after, when Freedling had become King in his father's stead, the fifth birthday of the Prince his son came to be celebrated; and there on the morning of the day, among all the presents that covered the

floor of the chamber, stood a beautiful foal rocking-horse, black, with deep-burning eyes.

No one knew how it had come there, or whose
present it was, till the King himself came to look at
it. And when he saw it so like the old Rollonde he
had loved as a boy, he smiled, and, stroking its dark
mane, said softly in its ear, "Art thou, then, the son
of Rollonde?" And the foal answered him, "Ah,
dear Prince and kind Master!" but never a word
more.

Then the King took the little Prince his son,
and told him the story of Rollonde as I have told it
here; and at the end he went and searched in the
foal's mane till he found one white hair, and
drawing it out, he wound it about the little Prince's
finger, bidding him guard it well and be ever a kind
master to Rollonde's son.

CANDY STOPS
A TRAIN

Christine Pullein-Thompson

Summer was nearly over and tomorrow a new school term would begin for the Fraser children. But when the telephone rang, school was the last thing they were thinking about.

A minute or so later, Mum came rushing into the kitchen. "Gran's had a fall," she told them. "She says she's all right, but she sounded rather peculiar on the phone. I must go over straight away."

The children began to interrupt with anxious questions, but Mrs Fraser cut them short. "I don't know any details," she said. "Liz, you're the eldest, so be sensible and look after the others. I'll ring your father and he'll come home from work."

The children were rather quiet when their mother had gone, because they were worried about their gran. But Liz decided that sitting about wouldn't do them any good. "Let's groom Candy," she suggested. Candy was the family pony.

They all ran outside, and climbed over the paddock gate. Then they stopped and stared. The paddock was empty! Candy wasn't there. It didn't take long to discover the broken rail in the fence, on which there were some of Candy's grey hairs.

Liz decided that they must first ring Gran's number, but no one answered the phone. "It may mean that Mum's taken Gran to hospital," said Liz. She decided to write Mum a note instead.

Candy's gone, it said. *We are looking for her. Will keep in contact. Love, Liz.*

She taped the note to the fridge door.

"Right!" she said. "Some bits of bread for Candy and then we're off!"

Neil picked up the headcollar and wound the rope round his waist.

"She must be up at the farm!" cried Liz hopefully. "Come on! Run!"

But there was no sign of Candy anywhere on the farm, and no one had seen her.

"What do we do now?" demanded Vicky.

"Go on searching!" replied Liz. "Neil, you go home, fetch the bike and look for her in the village. We'll go down Mole Lane. If you don't find her, follow us!"

So Neil returned to the cottage, while Liz and Vicky picked their way through the farmyard and into Mole Lane. It twisted and turned for miles, with high hedges on each side. Soon Vicky was tired.

"We aren't going to find Candy," she said. "Please, Liz, let's go home and wait for Mum."

But Liz just went on walking along the lane.

Neil had cycled all round the village, but there was no sign of Candy. It was as though she had evaporated into thin air.

Liz loved Candy more than anything in the world, except her family. She tried to imagine life without the little pony. Vicky wasn't as worried as Liz. She was sure that Mum would come back and be able to find Candy.

"Let's go home," she begged. "Candy isn't here. Anybody can see that."

"Just round one more corner," answered Liz. But when they reached the corner, they saw that the lane ahead was deserted. Behind them they heard the sound of Neil's bicycle bell, and they turned round, hoping that he was bringing good news.

But he only said, "No luck."

"Well that's that," said Liz, with awful finality in her voice. "We really ought to go home now!"

But Neil had thought of something.

"There's a level crossing further along this lane," he said. "You don't think —"

The children stared at each other, horrified at the picture going through their minds. Then Liz and Vicky started to run down the lane towards the railway line, while Neil pedalled along beside them.

"Oh please don't let her be there," Liz said silently to herself.

But she was. When the children reached the level crossing, Candy was standing on the railway line, munching the grass that grew alongside it. She managed to look happy and naughty at the same time. Liz realized that the pony wasn't at all anxious to go home.

She began to imagine the train rushing towards the crossing at a hundred miles an hour. She heard Neil calling: "Come on, Candy, come on! Good girl!" But he did not dare go on to the railway lines. Although no train was in sight, the lights by the crossing barriers might start flashing at any moment. A railwayman visiting Neil's school had said that there might be as little as twenty-seven seconds to get across once the lights started flashing.

Neil called again, desperately now, but the pony

merely whisked her tail and walked further away down the line.

Suddenly Liz knew what she had to do. There was a telephone by the crossing. She could ring the signalman and stop the train! She opened the telephone box, and shouted into the receiver: "Stop the train! There's a pony on the line at Mole Lane crossing."

A voice in her ear said: "I'll do everything I can, but the London train will reach the crossing in less than five minutes. Just keep off the line!"

Liz told the others, and Neil called to Candy again. But the pony didn't move. Suddenly everything was very still, with nothing but the distant throb of a combine harvester to break the silence.

Then the barrier lights at the crossing started flashing, first orange, then red. The bleepers sounded, and then the barriers came down slowly, as if by magic.

Liz put her hands over her eyes and prayed:

"God, please save Candy and all the people on the train."

Now they could see the train hurtling towards them, and Candy was still on the line. The little pony looked at the red barrier lights. Then she looked towards Neil with her legs still straddling the railway lines, and nickered softly to him as though to say: "All right, I'm ready to go home now."

The driver had begun to apply his brakes as soon as the lights in his cab warned him of danger. He could see the pony on the line ahead, and three children leaning towards it, rigid with fear. There was a loud grinding sound. Passengers fell forward from their seats. Then, with the train nearly upon her, Candy moved swiftly to join the children. The train stopped.

Neil pushed the headcollar over Candy's ears, as Vicky cried out: "It's all right. Everything's going to be all right!"

And Liz began to shake with relief as the driver jumped down from his cab and walked along the line to reassure his passengers. He then went over to the telephone box. When he had finished speaking to the signalman, Liz said,

"Thank you. We really are grateful."

"That's all right," replied the driver. "Just make sure it never happens again."

With Neil still holding Candy firmly by the headcollar, the children watched as the driver climbed back into his cab and the train drew away. Liz's knees were still wobbly. Neil was biting his nails, and Vicky was sucking her thumb — something she hadn't done for months.

They started back along the lane, and as they turned the first corner, they saw Mum cycling towards them. The children waved and began to shout. They told her everything that had happened as they went back home.

Mrs Fraser went pale as she listened. "It could have been a disaster," she cried. "Thank goodness you had the sense to ring the signalman. Well done!"

"How is Gran?" asked Liz.

"Suffering a mild concussion. She hit her head when she fell. But the doctor says she'll be all right after a few days' rest."

Later on that evening the children turned Candy into the paddock and watched her roll over and over in delight. Their fear was gone. The terrible memory of Candy on the railway line and the barrier lights flashing was already becoming blurred.

But Liz knew that they would never entirely forget what had almost happened that day.

THE HALLOWE'EN PONY

A French folktale retold by Robert D. San Souci

Grandmother put another log on the fire. Outside the little house, which was not far from the sea, the wind was howling so fiercely that it set the windows rattling. "Listen to that!" said the old woman. "There's a storm brewing for sure."

She stirred the coals in the fireplace with a heavy poker until the new log caught and began to blaze. Satisfied, she turned to her three grandsons, who were sitting on the floor gazing thoughtfully into the flames. "Besides," she added, "this is Hallowe'en. Witches are abroad tonight, and the goblins, who are their servants, are wandering about in all sorts of disguises, looking for children to snatch away."

But Tom, the eldest boy, said, "I won't stay here, frightened of a little wind and old stories. I promised Colette I'd call on her tonight. She swore she wouldn't get a wink of sleep, if I didn't visit her before the moon had gone down."

"I have to go and catch lobsters and crabs," said the middle boy, Louis. "Not all the witches and goblins in the world will keep me from that."

All three brothers announced they were going out for one reason or another and ignored the warnings of their grandmother. Only the youngest child hesitated a minute, when she said to him, "You stay with me, my little Richard, and I'll tell you stories of fairy lands and magic animals."

But he wanted to pick blackberries by the moonlight, and so he ran out after his brothers.

He caught up with them on the rise, beneath the old oak tree.

"Grandmother talks about wind and storm, but I've never seen the weather finer or the sky more clear," said Louis. "I'll bring home plenty of crabs and lobsters tonight."

"See how big the moon is," said Tom. "Perhaps I can coax Colette to go for a walk with me."

Then Richard, who was starting for the blackberry patch, suddenly cried, "Look!" and he pointed to a little black pony standing quietly at the foot of the hill.

"Oh, ho!" said Louis. "That's old Frederic's pony; it must have escaped from its stable and is going down for a drink at the horse pond."

"Now, now, my pretty little pony," said Tom, going up and patting the creature with his hand, "you mustn't run away; I'll lead you to the pond myself."

With these words, he jumped on the pony's back.

"Take me, too," called Louis, and his brother helped him up.

"Don't leave me behind!" cried Richard, and his brothers helped him mount. Soon all three were astride the little black pony, which waited patiently till they had settled themselves. Tom clung to the pony's neck; Louis held Tom's waist; and Richard held Louis's shirt.

"Now, giddup!" urged Tom, and the little pony headed directly for the horse pond.

On their way, each brother met a friend and invited him to mount the pony. Soon there were six boys, holding on to one another and laughing.

The pony didn't seem to mind the extra weight but pranced merrily along under the brilliant moon.

The faster it trotted, the more the boys enjoyed the fun. They dug their heels into the pony's sides and called out, "Gallop, little horse! You've got six of the bravest riders in the world on your back!"

Soon they were racing along through the grassy fields near the seashore. The wind rose, sending clouds scudding across the face of the moon and whipping the pony's long black mane back across the eyes of the boys in front. Very close now, they could hear the waves pounding against the rocky shore.

The pony did not mind the noise at all. Instead of going to the horse pond, he circled around and cantered rapidly toward the seashore.

Louis, the middle brother, began to regret his wish to catch crabs and lobsters, and Richard, the youngest, found that he was no longer interested in blackberries. Both held on to their seats on the pony that was galloping at breakneck speed down toward the beach.

The eldest boy, Tom, seized the madly charging pony by the mane and tried to make it turn around. But he tugged and pulled in vain, for the pony galloped, fast as the howling wind, straight on toward the sea, pausing only when the first waves splashed over its hoofs.

The six riders thought to slip off the pony's back, while it lingered at the water's edge; but they found they were stuck fast to the creature's back.

Then, rearing up once, the little black pony neighed loudly, ran back and forth through the sea foam gleefully, then suddenly charged into the billowing waves, while its riders cried out in terror.

"The pony is bewitched!" wailed Tom. "We should have listened to Grandmother's warning."

The pony advanced farther and farther into the sea; the waves rose higher and higher until they covered the children's heads and the pony vanished beneath the swells.

Some say the children were drowned; some say the goblin pony carried them to a strange city of coral and pearl at the bottom of the sea. But they were never seen on dry land again.

ANOTHER GIRL'S PONY

Ann de Gale

"Calm down, Josh," Lucy whispered. "I'm here now. I hate lightning, too. Let's be two scaredy-cats together."

Her dripping tee shirt nightie clung to her sides and Josh's mane felt clammy against her cheek. But at least she'd managed to coax him into his shelter in the corner of the field, before drying him down with straw, throwing his rug over him and talking to him about this and that until the stormed eased off.

Although he still shuddered at every distant rumble of thunder, Josh seemed to sense that the worst was over. "I don't blame you for panicking," Lucy said. "All by yourself out here. The thunder woke me, too."

"I'd better get back indoors now," she told him. "I'll come and see you before I go to school."

After one last hug, she left him. Waving as she clambered over the gate, she hurried across the gravelly driveway to her back door, hoping to tiptoe up to her bedroom unnoticed. Some chance! For there in the kitchen was her mother, grabbing her raincoat from its hook, her hair still unbrushed.

"Lucy! What's going on?" she cried. "I went into your room, thinking you'd be frightened, but you weren't there. And just look at you now – drenched to the skin!"

Kate the cat eyed them scornfully from the windowsill while Lucy babbled on about Josh and the storm.

"Dad and I must have slept through most of it," said Mum. "It's after seven, now. You'd better have a hot shower and explain the rest over breakfast."

Dad was seeing to the toast when Lucy stepped back into the kitchen, ten minutes later, buttoning her school shirt as she went. "What's all this?" he barked. "Out in the storm . . . *you*, the girl who's supposed to be terrified of lightning!"

"It was far worse for Josh," Lucy mumbled, making for her chair. "He was going berserk out there. He needed me."

"You won't be much good to him if you catch pneumonia," said Mum, pouring out orange juice.

Lucy wished they'd try to understand. "I told Melinda I'd take care of him," she protested. "I promised –"

Dad scowled. He hated it when she answered back. "It's you we're talking about now, Lucy. Forget Melinda."

"How can I?" Lucy stared at him, almost in tears. These days, wherever she went, whatever she did, there was always something to remind her that Josh's true owner was Melinda Mace, who was spending two months abroad with her parents. When they returned in ten days' time, Josh would be Melinda's pony again. If Lucy wanted to ride him – groom him, even – she would have to ask her friend's permission first.

Friend was not quite the right word. Melinda, who lived in the big house next door, was a few years older than Lucy. She was mad about clothes and her parents let her stay up late, watching television. Now they were allowing her to miss the start of the school term. Riding was the only interest she shared with Lucy, the difference being that while Melinda had a pony of her own, Lucy had to be content with lessons at the local stables, helping out there – and with Josh, sometimes – during holidays and weekends.

"Sorry, Lucy," said Dad. "I didn't mean to snap at you. You're doing a great job, caring for Josh, but you must try to look after yourself, too. All right?" He smiled at her.

"All right." Lucy managed a rather watery grin in return.

At school that morning, Lucy was scolded twice for dreaming, and at break she told her best friend, Kerry, about Josh and the storm. "It felt so strange, the two of us being scared together," she said. "It was as if we belonged to each other. But when Melinda gets back . . . oh, I'll miss Josh like mad."

"Surely she'll let you ride him sometimes," said Kerry. "After you've looked after him all this time – she must."

Lucy frowned. "Melinda has such funny moods. One minute she's quite friendly, the next she ignores me altogether."

"My mum calls her Princess Snooty," Kerry giggled. "She says Melinda never lets anyone forget she has a rich dad who buys her everything she wants."

"Even a gorgeous chestnut pony," Lucy sighed. "But at least Josh will still live in the field next

door. Melinda can't stop me seeing him . . . talking to him."

When her mother arrived outside school that afternoon, Lucy hurled herself into the car. "How's Josh?" she asked eagerly.

"Fine, I think," Mum replied. "He's seemed very quiet all day – never strayed far from his shelter. I've been rather busy, but I've kept an eye on him from the window."

Lucy smiled gratefully. It was because Mum had been brought up on a farm, and was well used to animals, that Melinda's parents had been willing for Lucy to look after Josh for them. Lucy did most of the work – grooming, cleaning tack and filling the water trough – but Mum was always there in the background, ready to take charge if necessary.

As soon as they reached home, Lucy scampered across the drive to Josh's field, putting two fingers between her lips and whistling twice. This was her signal, her way of telling him she was back. Usually, he trotted over, happy to see her, no doubt hoping for a chunk of apple or carrot.

But not today. Lucy stared in dismay as he stumbled towards her: slowly, falteringly, as if trying to keep one hoof off the ground. "J-Josh — what's wrong?" she cried worriedly. Then she shouted across to her mother, who was unloading her shopping from the car. "Mum! Come quickly. Something's happened to Josh. He's *lame!*"

Mum was alarmed, too. After making sure there was no jagged stone lurking in his hoof, she called Mr Platt, the vet, who arrived half an hour later. Talking soothingly to Josh, he examined his injured foreleg, while Lucy and her mother looked on, answering his questions as carefully as they could.

"I'm afraid he's strained a tendon," said Mr Platt at last. "It's quite serious, and almost certainly happened while he was careering around in the storm."

"He'll be all right, won't he?" Lucy asked, blinking and wiping a stray tear from her cheek.

"In time, I hope so," replied the vet. "But he'll need a lot of rest. No riding for at least three months."

Lucy listened hard as he talked to Mum about treatment, using words like *hosing* and *strapping*. Then he turned back to Josh, and spent quite a time bathing and bandaging his leg, before promising to return the next day.

"I know how you must feel," Mum said, hugging Lucy as they watched him drive away, "but Mr Platt's a wonderful vet – everyone says so. We must trust him and do everything he says. Now come and have some tea – I insist on that – and then you can stay with Josh until bedtime."

"But will he get better?" Lucy was speaking half to herself as she followed Mum indoors. "And what about Melinda? You know what she's like – she'll be so upset –"

"We're upset too," Mum interrupted gently. "I only hope she'll find time to give Josh all the care and love he'll need until he's fit again. We must help her as much as we can."

Lucy nodded uneasily, wondering what kind of

near-miracle was needed to change Princess Snooty overnight into a *caring* and *loving* person.

Over the next nine days, Lucy spent every spare moment with Josh, sitting on a bucket talking to him, and fetching and holding things for Mum while she carried out Mr Platt's orders. The pony was still lame but didn't seem to be in pain.

"Oh Josh," Lucy whispered, resting her head against his mane, the night before Melinda's return. "I don't care whether I ride you or not – I'll always love you. I'll come and talk to you every day, I promise."

When Lucy returned from school the following afternoon, the first person she saw was Melinda, striding through the field towards her, wearing smart pink leggings and a furious frown.

"What have you done to my pony?" she shouted.

Lucy gaped at her. "What – what do you mean?"

"You promised to look after him," Melinda growled accusingly. "I trusted you – and now look what's happened!"

Lucy could hardly believe what she was hearing. Was this girl actually blaming her for Josh's injury? Frantically, she began trying to explain, but Melinda refused to listen.

"Don't say it wasn't your fault – nobody ever stops telling me that – but it doesn't make things any better for me, does it?"

"I'm s-so sorry," Lucy mumbled, almost in tears. "But Josh is getting better every day – really he is."

"Huh!" Melinda snorted. "Think that if you like, but when Dad called the vet this afternoon, Mr Platt said it was possible that Josh would never be able to jump again. In three or four months' time he'll probably be fit for boring, gentle rides, but maybe nothing like jumping – ever."

Lucy sighed, wondering how anyone could talk so sneeringly about gentle rides on a dream of a pony like Josh.

"What good's that?" Melinda raged on. "It's not certain, but it sounds pretty dire to me. I need a

pony who jumps – one I can take to shows – and now I'm lumbered with Josh, a *cripple*! He'd be better off in an animal rest home."

Suddenly, Lucy could take no more. "Don't speak about him like that," she yelled. "Josh needs you now more than ever before. How can you treat him like some *thing* – some broken-down car that's ready for the scrap heap? You're selfish, Melinda – cruel!"

Sobbing, and without waiting for a reply, she raced home.

"It was horrible for you," her mother said, cuddling Lucy close and drying her tears with a tissue, "but it's my guess Melinda was still too shocked to know what she was saying. She'll feel differently in a day or two. Just give her time."

"But what if Josh is sent to a rest home," Lucy

wailed. "I'd never see him again — he might not like it there." She had never felt so miserable — or helpless — in all her life.

Two evenings later, when she knew Melinda was out at a party, Lucy spent almost an hour with Josh in the field. Just as she was saying goodnight, she heard a gruff voice behind her.

"Ah, Lucy — I thought I'd find you here."

She turned to see Melinda's father, Mr Mace, walking up to her, and wondered guiltily if he was cross with her for trespassing on his land. But then she saw the smile on his face.

"I've just had a talk with your dad," he began, "and he told me how you ran out into the storm, in spite of your terror of lightning. I suppose he was right to be angry, but Josh might have caused himself a far worse injury if you hadn't been there to calm him. You were very brave, Lucy."

Josh nuzzled Lucy's arm and she ran her fingers through his mane. "Not really," she said. "I just love him so much."

"I know you do," said Mr Mace, "and that's why I've come to ask if you'd like to carry on caring for him."

Lucy stared at him. "B–But Melinda said —"

"Never mind what she said," he cut in, laughing. "She's come to her senses now. She's even quite ashamed of herself. Of course she doesn't want Josh to go to a rest home — and nor do I. He's staying right here in this field and if you're willing to take him on as your own pony – ride him as soon as he's fit enough – that's fine by all of us, your parents included."

"Even Melinda?" Lucy asked doubtfully.

"Even Melinda." He pulled a funny face. "I know I spoil her, but she's really too heavy for Josh now, so I've promised her a bigger pony. It will be company for Josh, too. What do you say, Lucy?"

Lucy didn't know whether to laugh or to cry and had to struggle to say anything at all. "It's like a fairy story," she breathed. "Everything's terrible and hopeless – and then suddenly your impossible dream comes true."

She gazed at Josh and, from the happy gleam in his eye, she guessed he'd understood every single word they'd said.

THE HORSES
OF THE SUN

A Greek myth retold by Linda Jennings

Phaeton was the son of a sea nymph, Clymene. When he was a young boy, his mother would point to the sky, where the Sun God, Apollo, raced across the Heavens in his golden chariot.

"Apollo is your father, Phaeton," she told him.

The son of Apollo? Who would believe him? His friends certainly did not. They laughed at him, and said he was living in a land of dreams. In the end, Phaeton found it difficult to believe it himself.

"Very well," said Clymene. "If you think I am not telling you the truth, go to the Sun God and ask him yourself." Phaeton thought this was a very exciting idea. He saddled his horse and set off for the palace, which lay on the edge of the world.

When Phaeton at last arrived, he was dazzled by the golden splendour of Apollo's palace. He dismounted, and ran up the steps, shading his eyes against the brightness. He felt a little afraid. Would the Sun God greet him as a son, or throw him out as an intruder?

Phaeton tiptoed through marble halls and jewel-encrusted rooms, until he came to the Great Hall itself, where Apollo sat on his throne, attended by his servants, the Days and Months and Seasons of the year.

Apollo looked up, as Phaeton timidly approached the throne. He recognized his son immediately. He knew everything that happened on Earth, and had been watching over Phaeton throughout his childhood.

"I know what you have come to ask," he said. Phaeton had bowed his head, for he was afraid to look into the brilliant face of the Sun God. "And in answer to your question, yes, I *am* your father."

Phaeton was still unsure. How could this splendid god who galloped across the Heavens in his golden chariot be his father?

Apollo bent down, and put his hand on the boy's shoulder.

"You want proof?" he asked. "Then you shall have it. Because you are my son, I will grant you any wish you desire."

Any wish? Phaeton's heart beat fast. He knew exactly what he wanted, knew exactly how he could prove to his friends that he was Apollo's son!

"Let me drive your chariot across the skies for one whole day," he said.

Apollo groaned. "I would you had asked for anything but that. My horses are strong and fierce. Not even the King of the Gods, Zeus, dare drive them. You would not be able to control the chariot."

But Phaeton had one idea in his head, and one idea only. He felt breathless with excitement, as he thought of the four fiery horses, and how envious his friends would be, when they saw him racing across the skies.

"No, Father," he said. "There is nothing else I want from you. Please let me drive your chariot."

Apollo sighed, for he knew he could not persuade Phaeton to accept any other favour.

"If you insist, then I cannot stop you," he said. "But I fear it will end badly."

Phaeton was so impatient to be off, that he scarcely listened to his father's words. He ran behind Apollo as he strode through the palace, until they reached the stables.

Apollo flung open the doors, and Phaeton stepped back, blinking. The palace itself had been dazzling, but the chariot, which had been made by the Blacksmith God, Hephaistos, burned with a heat that hurt his eyes.

Apollo brought out the horses, and hitched them to the chariot. Jet-black they were, with glowing, red eyes. They tossed their proud heads, and showed their strong white teeth. Their golden hooves clashed on the marble floor, until sparks flew.

How fierce and uncontrollable they looked!

Phaeton trembled with fear, but then he thought of his mother and his friends, looking up into the skies, admiring his skill in controlling the four wild horses.

"Give me the reins, Father," he said. "I am ready."

"Dawn is nearly here," said Apollo. "Now listen to me. You must follow the path you see before you. Do not stray from it, for not only would you plunge to your death, but you would destroy the Earth itself."

Apollo watched his son climb into the chariot, and grasp hold of the reins, while the horses snorted and clashed their hooves. He felt great sadness, for he knew well enough that the boy was not strong enough to bring the horses and chariot safely home again.

"Goodbye, Father," called Phaeton, looking back at the Sun God as he drove off. "You'll be proud of me – you see!"

At first, Phaeton held on tightly to the reins. The horses, though, were used to Apollo's strength, and his firm commands. This slender young boy felt as light as a fly, and his voice was barely more than a whisper. They surged forward, and climbed steeply towards the summit of the Heavens.

"Wonderful!" cried Phaeton, as the horses sped on. "See me, Mother! See me, the son of Apollo!"

But very soon, things began to go wrong. As the horses snorted and plunged, the chariot swung from side to side. Phaeton clung to it, and looked over the edge. Below him he saw a terrible giant crab, waving its pincers, for he was passing through the signs of the Zodiac. He shut his eyes, and grasped the reins even more tightly, as the horses galloped wildly towards the summit.

Phaeton had been frightened before, but now he was terrified. What would happen when the horses began their downward journey?

He was soon to find out.

Down on Earth, it was midday, and up in the Heavens, Phaeton had reached the summit. He looked over the edge of the swaying chariot, and saw that the path ran almost vertically downwards. The horses reared up, then plunged, tugging the reins from Phaeton's hands. He cried out in fear, as the horses and chariot left the path altogether, and careered wildly towards Earth.

Poor Phaeton had not realized the destruction he would cause if he lost control of the horses. His eyes widened in horror as he saw the oceans dry up, and great fires rage across the land.

"Oh stop!" he cried. "Please, stop!"

He thought of his mother and his friends fleeing the fires, he thought of houses and crops being burned up. But the horses raced on. Their eyes glowed like rubies as they skimmed the surface of the Earth.

Zeus, the King of the Gods, lived on the top of Mount Olympus. He looked down in horror, as he saw the horses gallop out of control. He saw what Phaeton was doing to the Earth. He sent for Apollo, and told him that the boy must be stopped, before he destroyed Earth entirely.

Apollo wept as he thought of his son, terrified and alone but for the fierce, wild horses. But he knew that Zeus was right: Phaeton could not be allowed to go on.

Zeus took a thunderbolt, and hurled it at the chariot, which flew into a thousand pieces. Phaeton gave one last cry of terror, before he was flung down, down, into the river Eridus, where he drowned.

For a time, the Earth lay in darkness, for the sun chariot had vanished from the sky. Then Apollo rounded up the frightened horses, and took them back to the stables. Another chariot was hastily built, and Apollo once again began his daily journey across the Heavens.

The scorched Earth began to blossom again, and the birds to sing. Phaeton's mother had not been killed. She found the spot where her son had drowned, and she stayed there, day after day, weeping for his death. At last Apollo took pity on her, and changed her into an alder tree. The tree bent to the water, to kiss the drowned boy.

And the Sun God's reflection stayed with him, too, floating on the surface of the river.

THE CHRISTMAS PONY

Lincoln Steffens

What interested me in our new neighbour-hood was not the school, nor the room I was to have in the new house all to myself, but the stable which was built at the back of the house. My father let me direct the making of a stall, a little smaller than the other stalls, for my pony, and I prayed and hoped, and my sister Lou believed, that that meant that I would get the pony, perhaps for Christmas. I pointed out to her that there were three other stalls and no horses at all. This I said in order that she should answer it. She could not. My father, sounded out, said that some day we might have horses and a cow; meanwhile a stable added to the value of a house. "Some day" is a pain to a boy who lives in and knows only "now". My good little sisters, to comfort me, remarked that

Christmas was coming, but Christmas was always coming and grown-ups were always talking about it, asking you what you wanted and then giving you what they wanted you to have.

Though everybody knew what I wanted, I told them all again. My mother knew that I told God, too, every night. I wanted a pony, and to make sure they understood, I declared that I wanted nothing else.

"Nothing but a pony?" my father asked.

"Nothing," I said.

"Not even a pair of high boots?"

That was hard. I did want boots, but I stuck to the pony. "No, not even boots."

"Nor candy? There ought to be something to fill your stocking with, and Santa Claus can't put a pony into a stocking."

That was true, and he couldn't lead a pony down the chimney either. But no. "All I want is a pony," I said. "If I can't have a pony, give me nothing, nothing."

Now, I had been looking myself for the pony I wanted, going to sales stables, inquiring of horsemen, and I had seen several that would do. My father let me "try" them. I tried so many ponies that I was learning fast to sit a horse. I chose several, but my father always found some fault with them. I was in despair. When Christmas was at hand I had given up all hope of a pony, and on

Christmas Eve I hung up my stocking along with my sisters', of whom, by the way, I now had three.

I speculated on what I'd get. I hung up the biggest stocking I had, and we all went reluctantly to bed to wait until morning. Not to sleep; not right away. We were told that we must not only sleep promptly, we must not wake up until seven-thirty — if we did, we must not go to the fireplace for our Christmas. Impossible.

We did sleep that night, but we woke up at six a.m. We lay in our beds and debated through the open doors whether to obey until, say, half past six. Then we bolted. I don't know who started it, but there was a rush. We all disobeyed; we raced to disobey and get first to the fireplace in the front room downstairs. And there they were, the gifts, all sorts of wonderful things, mixed-up piles of presents; only, as I disentangled the mess, I saw that my stocking was empty; it hung limp; not a thing in it; and under and around it — nothing. My sisters had knelt down, each by her pile of gifts; they were squealing with delight, until they looked up and saw me standing there in my nightgown with nothing. They left their piles to come to me and look with me at my empty place. Nothing. They felt my stocking: nothing.

I don't remember whether I cried at that moment, but my sisters did. They ran with me back to my bed, and there we all cried until I became indignant. That helped some. I got up, dressed, and driving my sisters away, I went alone out into the yard, down to the stable, and there, all by myself, I wept. My mother came out to me by and by; she found me in my pony stall, sobbing on the floor, and she tried to comfort me. But I heard my father outside; he had come part way with her, and she was having some sort of angry quarrel with him. She tried to comfort me; besought me to come to breakfast. I could not; I wanted no comfort and no breakfast. She left me and went on into the house with sharp words for my father.

I don't know what kind of breakfast the family had. My sisters said it was "awful". They were ashamed to enjoy their own toys. They came to me, and I was rude. I ran away from them. I went around to the front of the house, sat down on the steps, and, the crying over, I ached. I was wronged, I was hurt − I can feel now what I felt then, and I am sure that if one could see the wounds upon our hearts, there would be found still upon mine a scar from that terrible Christmas morning. And my

father, the practical joker, he must have been hurt, too, a little. I saw him looking out of the window. He was watching me or something for an hour or two, drawing back the curtain ever so little lest I catch him, but I saw his face, and I think I can see now the anxiety upon it, the worried impatience.

After I don't know how long, surely an hour or two, I was brought to the climax of my agony by the sight of a man riding a pony down the street, a pony and a brand-new saddle; the most beautiful saddle I ever saw, and it was a boy's saddle; the man's feet were not in the stirrups; his legs were too long. The outfit was perfect; it was the realization of all my dreams, the answer to all my prayers. A fine new bridle, with a light curb bit. And the pony! As he drew near, I saw that the pony was really a small horse — what we called an Indian pony, a bay, with black mane and tail, and one white foot and a white star on his forehead. For such a horse as that I would have given, I could have given, anything.

But the man, a dishevelled fellow with a blackened eye and a fresh-cut face, came along, reading the numbers on the houses, and, as my hopes − my impossible hopes − rose, he looked at our door and passed by, he and the pony, and the saddle and the bridle. Too much. I fell upon the steps, and having wept before, I broke now into such a flood of tears that I was a floating wreck when I heard a voice.

"Say, kid," it said, "do you know a boy named Lennie Steffens?"

I looked up. It was the man on the pony, back again, at our horse block.

"Yes," I spluttered through my tears. "That's me." "Well," he said, "then this is your horse. I've been looking all over for you and your house. Why don't you put your number where it can be seen?"

"Get down," I said, running out to him.

He went on saying something about "ought to have got here at seven o'clock; told me to bring the nag here and tie him to your post and leave him for you. But I got into a drunk — and a fight — and a hospital — and —"

"Get down," I said.

He got down, and he boosted me up to the saddle. He offered to fit the stirrups to me, but I didn't want him to. I wanted to ride.

"What's the matter with you?" he said, angrily. "What you crying for? Don't you like the horse? He's a dandy, this horse. I know him of old. He's fine at cattle; he'll drive 'em alone."

I hardly heard, I could scarcely wait, but he persisted. He adjusted the stirrups, and then, finally, off I rode, slowly, at a walk, so happy, so thrilled, that I did not know what I was doing. I did not look back at the house or the man, I rode off up the street, taking note of everything — of the reins, of the pony's long mane, of the carved leather saddle. I had never known anything so beautiful. And mine! I was going to ride up past Miss Kay's house. But I noticed on the horn of the saddle some stains like raindrops, so I turned and trotted home, not to the house but to the stable. There was the family, father, mother, sisters, all working for me, all happy. They had been putting in place the tools of my new business: blankets, currycomb, brush, pitchfork – everything, and there was hay in the loft.

"What did you come back so soon for?" somebody asked. "Why didn't you go on riding?"

I pointed to the stains. "I wasn't going to get my new saddle rained on," I said. And my father laughed. "It isn't raining," he said. "Those are not raindrops."

"They are tears," my mother gasped, and she gave my father a look which sent him off to the house. Worse still, my mother offered to wipe away the tears still running out of my eyes. I gave her such a look as she had given him, and she went off

after my father, drying her own tears. My sisters remained and we all unsaddled the pony, put on his halter, led him to his stall, tied and fed him. It began really to rain; so all the rest of that memorable day we curried and combed that pony. The girls plaited his mane, forelock, and tail, while I pitchforked hay to him and curried and brushed, curried and brushed. For a change we brought him out to drink; we led him up and down, blanketed like a racehorse; we took turns at that. But the best, the most inexhaustible fun, was to clean him. When we went reluctantly to our midday Christmas dinner, we all smelt of horse, and my sisters had to wash their faces and hands. I was asked to, but I wouldn't until my mother bade me

look in the mirror. Then I washed up – quick. My face was caked with the muddy lines of tears that had coursed over my cheeks to my mouth. Having washed away that shame, I ate my dinner, and as I ate I grew hungrier and hungrier. It was my first meal that day, and as I filled up on the turkey and the stuffing, the cranberries and the pies, the fruit and the nuts – as I swelled, I could laugh. My mother said I still choked and sobbed now and then, but I laughed, too; I saw and enjoyed my sisters' presents until – I had to go out and attend to my pony, who was there, really and truly there, the promise, the beginning of a happy double life. And – I went and looked to make sure – there was the saddle, too, and the bridle.

But that Christmas, which my father had planned so carefully, was it the best or the worst I ever knew? He often asked me that; I never could answer as a boy. I think now that it was both. It covered the whole distance from broken-hearted misery to bursting happiness – too fast. A grown-up could hardly have stood it.

SWALLOW

Julie Sykes

Amy lived with her mum and dad on a farm. There weren't any other houses nearby and Amy often got lonely. At half-term Dad took Amy to market with him. She was allowed to help unload the calves from the trailer and when the calves were settled in the stalls Dad told Amy she could look around the market on her own.

"I've some business to see to but it won't take long. Don't wander outside the market gates."

It was fun walking around the market. Amy liked animals and wished she could have a pet. Although there were lots of animals on the farm, they all had jobs to do, even the cats who slept in the barn and kept the mice down.

Looking at the horses Amy was surprised at how large some of them were. Dad didn't have horses on their farm, so she had never seen them at close hand. She had just decided she liked the little ones the best, for she wasn't very big herself, when someone called out her name. Amy turned round and her stomach cartwheeled. Behind her stood a man whom she recognized. His name was Mr Parson and he was known locally as the slaughter man. Sometimes, if an animal was very sick, he came to the farm. Amy always hid until he had gone as it upset her to see him take their animals away.

Mr Parson leant over a stall and patted a pony on the rump, saying:

"I'll be seeing you later." He smiled at Amy and briskly walked away.

Amy shivered as she leant over the stall to look at the pony inside. The poor thing was nothing but bones. Its coat was caked with dirt and its mane and tail matted with burrs.

"Poor pony," Amy whispered and reached out to stroke its nose. The pony eyed her nervously.

"Don't be afraid. I'm not going to hurt you."

Very gently, Amy ran her hand along the pony's neck. Slowly, the animal began to relax and then it nuzzled her arm.

Amy had never touched a horse before and it was a wonderful feeling. Suddenly she had an idea. She gave the pony one last pat then ran off to find Dad.

Dad's business had gone well and he was in a good mood. He let Amy drag him back to see the horses. But when she showed him the little pony he was puzzled.

"I want you to buy it," said Amy firmly.

Dad rubbed his chin before answering.

"There's no room for pets on the farm Amy, you know that."

"Please Dad," Amy begged.

Dad was amused. "But it's such a sick-looking thing. What use would it be?"

"It would be company for me," said Amy. "And if you don't buy it Mr Parson will." She stuck her chin out and stared at him with her huge green eyes.

Dad knew that look, Amy had a very determined streak. He smiled to himself. Why not indulge her this once? It would be company for her and give her a sense of responsibility.

"Come on then," he smiled. "Let's see what we can do."

When the bidding for the little pony started Amy could hardly bear to watch for she was sure Mr Parson would win. She couldn't believe her good luck when the auctioneer pointed his hammer at Dad and said:

"Sold."

Amy let her breath rush out in a noisy sigh of relief.

Dad wasn't sure how they were going to get the pony home but on the way to collect her they bumped into a farmer from a neighbouring farm. Tom Butler had come to market to sell his hunter and willingly agreed to transport Amy's pony back home in his horse box. At first, Amy felt shy about travelling with Mr Butler, but her shyness soon vanished when she tried to lead the pony into the horse box. The pony was very frightened and she rolled her eyes and snorted in alarm.

"Steady." Gently Amy stroked the pony's neck. "Come on, I won't hurt you."

As she talked, Amy started to walk inside the horse box, allowing the rope between her and the pony to lengthen. Suddenly, as if realizing she would be left behind, the pony started forward and followed Amy inside.

"Good girl, that wasn't so bad was it?" Amy was triumphant as she tied her pony up.

It was only a short ride home and when they drove into the yard Amy rushed indoors to find Mum.

"Come and see what I've got," she shouted. "Dad rescued her from the slaughter man and Mr Butler brought her home."

Safe in the horse box the little pony didn't want to come out again. She trembled and refused to move. Amy talked to her while softly stroking her head. Gradually the trembling stopped and she followed Amy down the ramp.

"A pony!" exclaimed Mum, coming out of the house to see why Amy had shouted at her. "What a good idea. That will keep you out of mischief!"

After thanking Mr Butler for the ride home, Amy made her new pony a thick bed of straw in one of the cow pens. In the corner she left a fresh bucket of water and a large net of hay.

"Tomorrow I'll go to the feed supplier and buy some pony nuts," Dad promised.

"And I will think of a name for you," said Amy patting her new friend goodbye.

Over tea, Mum made another suggestion.

"Auntie Sarah used to have horses once. We could ask her to come over and take a look at your new pony."

Auntie Sarah was Mum's sister and she lived in the village where Amy went to school.

The following day Dad went to buy the pony nuts and came back with grooming brushes as well. Amy was so delighted she spent the rest of the day getting the dirt out of the pony's coat and

untangling her mane and tail. It was hard work but she didn't mind. She liked being busy and it was fun having someone real to talk to.

"You're going to be the prettiest pony for miles," she told her. The pony snorted and tossed her head. Under the dirt she was a lovely chocolate brown, with a white patch on her forehead that looked like a bird.

As soon as she saw it Amy knew what to call her new friend: Swallow. It was a perfect name!

Mum phoned Auntie Sarah and invited her over. When she arrived, Amy took her straight to the cow barn. Auntie Sarah examined Swallow closely without saying anything. Amy held her breath. She loved Swallow and wanted her aunt to love her too.

"She's too thin," said Auntie Sarah at last. "But she's got good bones. I'll give you a special diet for her, and when she's fatter I'll teach you how to ride."

Amy beamed and put her arms around Swallow's soft neck.

Before she left, Auntie Sarah wrote down a list of foods to fatten the pony up. She handed it to Amy saying, "By the time I come to stay in the summer holidays Swallow should be fit enough for you to ride her."

Amy was surprised. No one had told her that Auntie Sarah was coming to stay in the summer.

But when she asked questions about the visit, her aunt changed the subject.

Over the following weeks Amy spent all her free time looking after Swallow. Gradually the pony filled out, and her coat shone from regular grooming. Amy moved her to Home Field where the grass was long and green and when Swallow saw her coming, she would run to the gate and whicker.

As Swallow grew, Dad teased Amy. "If that pony gets any larger she'll be too fat for you to ride her."

Swallow was getting fat. Her belly was as round as a barrel, and although Amy cut down her pony nuts, still she grew. Amy often took Swallow for a walk in the headcollar and lead rein she had bought with her pocket money. Amy would chatter away, telling the little mare about school and sharing secrets with her. In return Swallow would whicker and rub her head on Amy's arm. One day, when Amy had taken Swallow up to the top field, they saw one of the barn cats climbing into a hollow in a tree. Curious, Amy peered in after her and found a nest of kittens. They were very young, with tightly closed eyes.

That night Amy lay in bed thinking about Swallow, for she was still getting fat. A wonderful thought stole into her mind. When she next groomed Swallow Amy was extra careful with her stomach. She couldn't wait for Auntie Sarah to visit again.

Auntie Sarah arrived unexpectedly the following weekend. Proudly Amy took her outside to see Swallow.

"Goodness me," exclaimed Auntie Sarah. "Is this the same pony?"

Amy laughed. Her hard work had paid off. Swallow did look like a different horse.

"I'm sorry Amy, but you can't ride her like this," Auntie Sarah continued.

So she had been right! Amy was so excited she felt as if she would burst.

"She's going to have a foal isn't she?" she asked.

Auntie Sarah looked at Amy in surprise. Swallow wasn't going to have a foal, she was just too fat to be ridden. From her car her aunt pulled out a second-hand saddle. When she put it on the pony's back the girth was too short to fit around her belly.

"Too much grass," said Auntie Sarah firmly. "You

will have to put her in the cow barn to stop her eating so much."

At first Amy was very disappointed. She had been sure Swallow was going to have a foal and in her mind she had planned all the things the three of them would do together. It would have been fun having a foal to look after. The new saddle and bridle helped to lessen her disappointment, though, especially when Auntie Sarah showed her how to clean them. The summer holidays were getting closer, and if Swallow lost some weight Amy could start riding her then. Showing Swallow the tack she said sternly, "You've got to go on a diet."

Swallow snorted and tossed her head. Amy giggled. She was sure Swallow could understand her.

"We'll start tomorrow," she said, and gave the pony a lump of sugar.

"No wonder she's so fat," Auntie Sarah scolded.

Auntie Sarah stayed for tea and after the meal Amy told Mum and Dad about Swallow's diet.

"I thought she was having a foal," she finished.

No one laughed. Mum looked at Dad and Auntie Sarah stared at the ceiling. Then Dad said, "I think we should tell her."

"Tell me what?" asked Amy.

Mum smiled and patted her stomach. "There is going to be a baby after all! I'm having one."

Amy didn't know what to say. She'd often wondered what it would be like to have a brother

or sister, now she was going to find out. She jumped up and threw her arms around her mother.

"That's even better than having a foal."

Everyone laughed and hugged each other.

After Auntie Sarah had left, Amy went out to say goodnight to Swallow. The little pony nuzzled her head against Amy's arm and Amy told her about the new baby. For once, Amy was really looking forward to the long summer holiday. She patted Swallow's smooth brown neck, then ran indoors to bed.